LEGACY

THEYTUS BOOKS

Library and Archives Canada Cataloguing in Publication

Rice, Waubgeshig, 1979-, author

Legacy / Waubgeshig Rice.

ISBN 978-1-926886-34-3 (pbk.)

I. Title.

PS8635.I246L44 2014   C813'.6   C2014-903432-6

Printed in Canada by Friesens

THEYTUS BOOKS

Publishing Indigenous Voices
Cover Design: Amber Allison
Edited by Adeena Karasick
Published by Theytus Books
www.theytus.com

 Patrimoine Canadian
canadien Heritage

 Canada Council Conseil des Arts
for the Arts du Canada

 BRITISH COLUMBIA
ARTS COUNCIL
Supported by the Province of British Columbia

 ONTARIO ARTS COUNCIL
CONSEIL DES ARTS DE L'ONTARIO
an Ontario government agency
un organisme du gouvernement de l'Ontario

We acknowledge the financial support of The Government of Canada through the Department of Canadian heritage for our publishing activities. We acknowledge the support of the Canada Council for the Arts, which last year invested $157 million to bring the arts to Canadians throughout the country. *Nous remercions le Conseil des arts du Canada de son soutien. L'an dernier, le Conseil a investi 157 millions de dollars pour mettre de l'art dans la vie des Canadiennes et des Canadiens de tout le pays.* We acknowledge the support of the Province of British Columbia through the British Columbia Arts Council

Dedicated to the Rice and Shipman families

Acknowledgements

The author would like to acknowledge the following for their support in making this book happen, and for their encouragement on this journey:

Canada Council for the Arts, Ontario Arts Council, Canadian Broadcasting Corporation, Paul Seesequasis, Adeena Karasick, Karen Waite, Sarah McGregor, Leanne Simpson, Richard Wagamese, Shelagh Rogers, Richard Van Camp, Jordan & Kim Wheeler, Cherie Dimaline, Susan Blight, Lee Maracle, Ann Doyon, Vera Wabegijig, Joseph Boyden, Ryan McMahon, Wab Kinew, Erinn Wright, Matt Peltomaki, Richard Larson, Ian Kerr, Matt McGregor, A Tribe Called Red, Niigaanwewidam Sinclair, Melissa Bailey-Bean, Thom Bennett, Charlotte Stein, Connie Walker, Melody McKiver, Vince & Anita Chechock, The Odawa Native Friendship Centre, Parry Sound High School, Wasauksing First Nation, Mario Carlucci, Kelly Hughes, Rosanna Deerchild, Katherena Vermette, Duncan Mercredi, Geoff Thomlinson, Sarah Labrie, Harvey & Sharon McCue, Digging Roots, Johna Hupfield, Maria Hupfield, Andrea Landry, Jorge Vallejos, Leonard Sumner, Alex Freedman, Ashley Wright, Octopus Books, Maria Morrison, Chris Jakins, Cecil Rosner.

LEGACY

Waubgeshig Rice

EVA
Winter 1989

The early March snow fell at a steady and silent pace on the downtown Toronto streets. Thick, cold white flakes fluttered from the low clouds and gently blanketed the concrete sidewalks and pavement. Cars, trucks, buses and streetcars roared along Spadina Avenue unheeded, but the people on foot couldn't ignore the winter precipitation. Their paces got slower and smaller as they stepped through the slippery and unpredictable frozen ground. Some of the young women walking south from the University of Toronto pulled scarves and hoods over their permed hair as the snow fell steadily upon them. They pulled their puffy, colourful parkas close and zipped them up. But one with long, straight black hair stood out, even in the multicultural parade of modern urban youth. A smile broke on her light brown face as the big flakes collected in her hair.

Heavy snowfall reminded Eva Gibson of home. She grew up on the Birchbark Indian Reserve on the north shore of Lake Huron, almost halfway between Sudbury and Sault Ste. Marie, Ontario. Her community got a lot of lake-effect snow every winter, and it cascaded densely like this when it wasn't windy-like a clean bedsheet whipped up with two hands and left to fall softly and evenly over a bare mattress. It didn't snow as often in the big city, but for Eva, whenever it happened it seemed to soften a lot of the harsher edges of urban life in the *white* world. As she strolled down the street, she looked up at the sky and inhaled deeply through her nostrils, trying to ignore the faint smell of exhaust fumes from the dozens of vehicles that sped by every few seconds.

Eva was a foreigner on these streets. Although people like her ancestors had navigated the rivers, streams and hills around what came to be known as Lake Ontario for thousands of years, she always felt uncomfortable and out of place in the city. Six months into her first year of university, though, she was feeling better. She negotiated the subways and streetcars with ease. The loud sirens didn't wake her up in the middle of the night anymore. She began to walk with a commanding pace on the city streets, head up. She had made a good handful of friends, both Native and non-Native. She got homesick from time to time, but her reserve was only a four hour bus ride north. All of her siblings, aunts and uncles, and dozens of cousins still lived there. In just two short months, she'd be back there for the summer and she was already eagerly awaiting the day her brothers came to pick her up to go back home.

Memories, aspirations, and snow were a brief distraction from Eva's hectic undergrad workload on this walk back to her student residence. Before the onslaught of finals, a pile of term papers were due, in everything from economics to political science to Canadian studies. She was in a general bachelor of arts program at U of T, and she hadn't yet decided on a major. One thing was clear, though: as soon as she got her B.A., she was set on going to law school. She decided back in high school that she was going to be a lawyer. She would learn about the law, and go back to her home community one day to work for her people. She wasn't sure how, but she would use her credentials to her community's advantage. No one in her family had ever graduated from a post-secondary education program, and she was determined to get multiple pieces of paper authorizing her success.

Eva continued down the busy sidewalk, as essay topics and deadlines flooded back into her mind. The snow that accumulated on the street was already turning brown and grey, as cars and trucks zooming past pushed it up against the curb. As she got closer to College Street, both the vehicle and pedestrian traffic picked up with the lunchtime rush. Boxy sedans and minivans from dark brown to yellow zipped past, while men with moustaches and thick, mulleted hair in tight light grey and blue business suits approached on the sidewalk. This was her cue to get off Spadina and head east on one of the quieter side streets to her residence.

Before long, she was darting up the concrete steps of her building. It was a three-story, red brick student dorm with big windows on the outskirts of campus that housed a little more than one hundred first-year students. Unlike some of the other older and more established university residences, it lacked ivy crawling up the outer walls and other affluent hints. It was much more modest, but it suited Eva just fine. She pulled open the heavy wooden door, stepped inside and stomped her insulated black boots on the mat. She slid her backpack off her arm, opened it, and rummaged through to get her wallet. She pulled it out and opened it to flash her student I.D. card to the security guard at the front desk. He nodded and she walked past him, up the stairs to the third floor.

As Eva climbed the carpeted steps to her room, she planned out the rest of her study routine for the day. It was Wednesday, and while most of her peers in residence were already looking towards their party plans for the weekend, she was determined to get one of her term papers done, and celebrate later. It was late in the afternoon, getting close to supper, and she hoped her roommate Melissa wasn't in their shared space. Melissa could be a bad influence this late in the day, and twist her arm into some kind of distraction, like going out to a movie or playing pool. Like Eva, she was also a general arts student from an Ojibway reserve in the north. Because they were the only two Native girls in the whole residence system, the administration placed them together under the premise that with common backgrounds, it would be easier for them to settle in to city life together. While they became good friends, their pairing in residence mostly just isolated them from the other non-Native students. They were still friends with others in their building and in their classes, but bridges between cultures weren't exactly under construction.

She turned right at the top of the stairs and walked down the hall to room 314. The hall was empty, but music and chatter echoed from a few open doors. Stacy and Vanessa were talking in the first room on the left. "Hey Eva!" they chirped simultaneously as they saw her pass. Eva smiled and waved politely. She generally tuned them out, but Nancy was playing the latest Poison album a little too loudly. Exhausted, all Eva could focus on was making it to her own shelter. The door was closed, so she could only assume Melissa was either in the library, the Native student lounge, or hanging out at their usual coffee spot on campus.

Relieved, she unlocked the door, walked in the room, threw

her backpack on the floor, turned and collapsed onto the bed. Her long, dark hair sprawled across the red and black quilt her grandmother made her as a child. She stared up at the white stuccoed ceiling, her hair spiralling around her head like a brunette vortex. She inhaled deeply through her nose and closed her eyes. Images of wide, yellow beaches sheltered by deep green pine and spruce trees with loud waves lapping the shore undulated through her. During those brief moments of refuge and solitude, her thoughts always wandered to home.

Eva always thought about that beach on the north shore of Lake Huron. It was the crown jewel of her community. Birchbark's boundary went from just below Highway 17 all the way down to the water—about a forty-five minute walk from the loud passage to the outside world to natural solitude. She felt fortunate to have grown up in a place that was still closely connected to the essence of Mother Earth. The beach stretched nearly a kilometre from end to end, enclosed by rocky terrain and tall trees on either side. Evergreens competed with oak and maple trees along the ridge behind the beach for the sun's attention. Looking south, small islands and the northern shoreline of Manitoulin Island were visible. All these elements combined made for the prototypical snapshot of the Great Lakes experience.

It was often windy in the summer, but it was always warm, and most of the time kids of all ages from the community could be found there swimming. It was loud, but still peaceful. At that oasis, everyone seemed to forget about the problems in their community. The dilapidated homes. The unstable leadership. The booze. At the beach, all of that went away, temporarily. As Eva daydreamed about her favourite spot in the world, lying on that hard single mattress in her downtown Toronto dorm room, her thoughts slowly drifted to her mother.

They were building sandcastles on the beach. Eva had three buckets: a small yellow one, a mid-sized red one, and a big blue one. She filled each using a small plastic shovel. She was wearing a pink bathing suit. Her black hair was tied back, still wet after emerging from the water just a few minutes before. She looked up at her mother, squinting at the sun behind her, and gave her a front-toothless smile. Eva could only see the silhouette of her mother's wide brimmed straw hat, but as she moved into her shadow, she saw her bright smile elevate her big Ojibway cheeks below round, dark sunglasses. Sitting in her plastic chair, Clara Gibson was wearing a light, white button-up short-sleeved shirt tucked into beige shorts that rested high on her waist. Her summer straw hat contained her short, curly hair.

"Mommy, how big should I make this one?" asked Eva.

"As big as you want, my girl," replied Clara. "You see all the sand on the beach here? This is all ours to share, but it's yours to use however you want."

"I'm gonna make us a big house to live in."

"Well you better get started before your dad gets home! He's gonna be hungry. Better start on the kitchen first!"

Eva faked a startled look, then began to giggle, masking her smirk with the plastic shovel. Clara bellowed a loud laugh, throwing her head back. For a few moments, the waves crashed harder into the shore, but at a steady, soothing pace. Clara looked out into the vast blue lake. The sun reflected sharp, white morsels of light off the rapidly heaving water, almost like it was pulling jewels deep out of the rocky floor beneath and bringing them to the top. It was already alive and blessing the mother and daughter with solitude and rejuvenation, but the wind and the sun seemed to enhance that brilliant spirit even more. Clara looked back down at Eva.

"My girl, I know we're not always happy at home. I know it's hard sometimes. It might get even harder for you while you're growing up. But I want you to know this will always be here for you. You will always have home. They can't take this away from us. Don't you forget this sand or this water. They are special gifts."

Eva's smile disappeared at the sudden seriousness of her mother's tone. She looked down at the yellow bucket and nodded. "I know, mommy," she said. "I won't never leave."

A tear rolled down from Eva's eye and pooled in her ear as she lay flat on her dorm room bed. She turned her head to the left, shook another tear loose from her other eye and took a deep breath to keep herself from sobbing. She brought herself up onto the bed and curled into a fetal position, as the image of the beach began to dissolve against the backs of her eyelids. The perpendicular pattern of the quilt was skewed now, as her body nestled into itself. She sniffled and bit her bottom lip. She missed her parents terribly, especially her mother.

Eva didn't want to feel sorry for herself. She didn't want her homesickness or her past to overcome her while she was here in Toronto for school. She resolved to only return home for good once she got her Law degree. People left Birchbark for different reasons. Some were running away from bad things, and they never came back. People like that usually went to far away places like Toronto or Winnipeg, or even Vancouver. Her childhood friend Danielle went to live with foster parents out West after her dad beat up her mom and went to jail. Eva hadn't seen her since they were twelve. Her cousin Carl took off to Toronto when he was sixteen. Everyone suspected their great uncle Jimmy molested him. She always wondered if she would see him down at Queen and Bathurst, where a lot of the Native street people hung out. She hadn't yet.

Then there were the few people who left to try to get an education. They were split into two distinct groups: the ones who made it, and the ones who didn't. The successful ones usually stayed in the cities where they studied. Carrie Eagle went all the way down to Windsor to study business about ten years earlier. As far as anyone knew, she only came back to see her parents and her sisters a couple times since. Eva wasn't sure what kind of job she had. Vince Pelletier left for Barrie to become a cop. He did really well and got a job there right away. He married a white woman and they only came to visit once after that, much to the disappointment of everyone else in Birchbark. People really liked him and they thought he would have made a good rez cop.

The majority of people who left for college or university,

though, were usually back within months or even weeks of starting. Over the past decade she could think of a handful of people who returned home, defeated by the outside world. Her eldest brother Edgar went to Ottawa to study Political Science, but he was back by Christmas of that year. She remembered him being very quiet and depressed in the months that followed. He started drinking a lot too. Another young man with whom she graduated high school, Danny King, came home from college in London at Thanksgiving and never went back. Despite all these stories that seemed to surround her, Eva promised herself she would stick it out. Not to prove to others that she was stronger or better; she just knew the accomplishment would be worth it. She understood the desire to go back home. It's hard for anyone from the North being way down in the Big Smoke, but it's especially hard as an Indian.

The cities most people migrated to were either Sudbury or Sault Ste. Marie. But as far as Eva was concerned, those migrations didn't really count, because Birchbark was roughly equal distance from both cities and the more significant Native populations in each made it easier to fit in. Some were lucky to get jobs in the nickel mine near Sudbury. Others moved to the Soo just because there were more reserves in the area. Either way, most people from Birchbark made day trips to either city for shopping or other adventures, so it wasn't a huge departure from the rez.

Eva caught herself. She didn't like putting the people she knew into categories like that. It seemed too academic, something her professors would do and then analyze to death. She also considered it to be a little judgmental. She wanted to try her best to stay humble here. That's what her grandparents taught her and she didn't want to think of herself any different from anyone else she grew up with. That humility is important in working together as a community, she thought. We'll all be able to take advantage of these opportunities someday, she hoped.

That introspective reflection was interrupted by the sharp sliding of a key into the lock in the door. Eva shot up quickly to sit on her bed, before the key turned and the door opened.

Melissa walked in, shaking the last few flakes of snow from her curly dark brown hair. "Aaaaaniiiiii!" she bellowed. "Holy, it's really coming down out there eh?" The slow, northern drawl of Melissa's rez accent was much stronger than Eva's. She grew up on a reserve on Manitoulin Island—not far from where Eva grew up—but being tucked away in a much bigger community and being from a much bigger family gave Melissa's voice that distinct Ojibway twang.

"I think it's kinda nice," replied Eva. "Reminds me of all that lake snow back home." Melissa took off her pink parka and hung it on the door. "Yeah I guess," said Melissa. "But this is the south! We're not supposed to get snow here!" She followed that up with a deep belly laugh. Eva chuckled too.

As Melissa peeled off her winter layers, Eva leaned over to reach her backpack on the floor and pulled out two big three-ring binders—a red one and a green one—and set them on her desk just at the foot of her bed. She then rummaged around for the textbooks of the classes she had that day: *Introduction to Microeconomics* and *Classic Philosophical Thought*. Lastly, she dug to the bottom to retrieve *The Dead* by James Joyce, which she was reading for her English class. She piled them on the desk and planned to leave them there for at least a few hours. Wednesday was her least favourite day for classes. Economics and the musings of ancient Greek philosophers didn't exactly hit home for her, but she knew these were academic foundations she couldn't ignore.

She loved English class, though. As a kid on Birchbark, she read a lot to pass the time, and to try to stay out of trouble. Like most young girls, she escaped into books at age twelve with the *Sweet Valley High* series, but her tastes eventually evolved into more mature titles by authors like V.C. Andrews. Here at university, she loved being able to dissect sentences and analyze words, tropes, and codes in search of something much deeper.

"How was class today?" asked Melissa, as she kicked off her boots and turned to the mirror.

"Alright. Economics is friggin' boring though!" replied Eva. "I don't even know why you take that!"

"I know."

Melissa grabbed a hairbrush from her own desk. Their sides of the room mirrored each other. The heads of their beds were pointed toward the window, with a night stand on the left of Eva's and another on the right of Melissa's. At the foot of each bed there was a desk, followed by a dresser and a closet. Melissa's curly hair was frizzy thanks to the moisture, so she turned to the mirror to brush it out. Her face was round, with high and chubby cheeks that made her squinty brown eyes disappear when she smiled. She wasn't a big girl, but appeared a little chubbier juxtaposed against Eva's tall and slender physique. Her hair was also much shorter and curlier than Eva's. Despite these physical differences, they were still seen as the same around campus; simply referred to as "the Indian Girls" both within and outside their circles of friends. That didn't really bother them that much, though, because at least they had each other.

Once her hair was a little more under control, Melissa turned to her bed and fell into it, face-first. "Uggghhh, I got so much work to do!" her muffled voice came from the pillow. "I hate this bullshit!"

"Me too geez," said Eva. "I just wanna get it over with and go home."

"Well, just another month and a bit to go."

"Did your uncle get you that job on your rez for the summer?"

"I dunno yet, he's supposed to call me sometime next week. What are you gonna do?"

"No idea, shit. Probably go back to Henry's."

Eva spent the summer before waitressing at a fish restaurant on the highway. Because so many tourists go through that part of the north shore, it was a great way to make tips. It also helped her come out of her shell a bit. She was a little shy as a kid and a teenager, but having to deal with so many strangers every day —especially non-Native people—prepared her for the transition into the big city.

Melissa turned and sat almost upright to face Eva, with her back leaning against the wall. "Well you said that's real good for tips eh?" she asked.

"Yeah, plus I can walk there from Edgar's place."

"How long does that take?"

"Only about a half hour. The only tricky part is crossing the highway when it's busy. But it's not bad."

The young women became quiet, more out of exhaustion than out of boredom or running out of things to say. Melissa was also in a General Arts program, but she was leaning more towards Social Work. Like Eva, she was using this first year to get settled. She was louder and a little more outgoing, and her social skills helped bring both of them into non-Native peer circles. Sometimes the other girls in the building or other students in their classes would invite them out. But most of the time Eva and Melissa were most comfortable in their own room, talking about the unique Native life that was familiar to them, yet largely alien to the people around them in Toronto.

Melissa crawled up to her pillow. "I'm gonna have a nap," she proclaimed, and turned to face the wall. Eva wasn't keeping track of how long she herself had been lying there, so she figured it was time to do some homework and start chipping away at that Political Science essay. It was due in a week. She stood up from her bed and took a couple of steps over to her desk and sat down. It was all very neatly organized: the books she just removed from her bag piled on the left, a desk lamp on the shelf above it, a stack of library books on the right, a mug full of pens and pencils in the far right corner, and above that—a family photo.

It was the most recent—and last—Gibson family photo. They posed for it at her cousin Debbie's wedding three years earlier in Birchbark. In the shot, all five children stand around their parents, William and Clara, who are seated. The backdrop is a lush natural green awning of oak and maple leaves. They're facing the sun, so they're all squinting—more so than the natural Ojibway squint they were all born with. The children are lined up behind the parents in order of age.

On the left is Edgar, the eldest. His white shirt with a thin, brown plaid pattern is tucked into his tight jeans. His hands are clasped at his waist, and a thick plume of dark brown hair hangs into his eyes. He smiles the widest, baring big white teeth. To the right is Norman, a year younger than Edgar and about two inches taller. He's wearing a plaid blue shirt, and his hair is short on the top and long at the back: the prototypical Native mullet. He smirks slightly, with his right hand on his father Bill's right shoulder.

In the middle is Eva, three years younger than Norman, and nearly as tall as him even back then. For some reason, her cousin Debbie convinced her to perm her hair leading up to the wedding, and looking back she remembered not liking it at all. She did love that white dress though. Eva always thought she appeared the focal point in this picture, which she was mildly ashamed of, but she did enjoy being nestled between her two seated parents.

To the right of Eva in the picture is her brother Stanley, two years younger than her and as awkward and lanky as ever. Already slightly taller than his two older brothers, his skinny arms shoot down from the short sleeves of his red polo shirt, while his left hand rests on his mother's left shoulder. His slender face is largely concealed by big, round glasses ("Indian Affairs" glasses, as most people called them), while his curly mullet drapes over his shoulders. This picture of Stanley always made Eva giggle. On the end, the Gibson kids are rounded out by Maria, a year younger than Stanley, and looking sharp in a blue summer dress. Her hair is artificially curly too, and her wide smile flashes thick braces.

Eva looked at this picture every day. And every day, her eyes eventually gravitated to her parents in the middle of the shot, and lingered there as sorrow and nostalgia crept up the back of her neck like malevolent vines. In that last family photo, Bill's smile makes his cheeks bunch high on his face, pushing the thick, large glasses up slightly past his eyebrows. His black hair looks thick and curly, and from a photographer's distance, the few grey hairs Eva remembers are invisible. His purple dress shirt fits tightly across his broad shoulders and over his middle-aged gut. His hands are placed neatly, palms-down on his thighs.

The family matriarch sits poised in the photo: back straight, shoulders back, chin up. Almost too elegant for the rez. Her cream-coloured dress seems to accentuate her dark brown arms and face. Clara also had a round, Great Lakes-Ojibway face, but she smiled only slightly with her lips tight together, keeping a symmetrical and striking visage. Her shoulder-length black hair is permed into small curls, a standard "mom" hair style for the time. Her chin is tilted slightly upward, and her slanted brown eyes seem to peer through the photographer himself, and through the years that passed since this photo was taken. Her grace is immortal.

Remembering was always bittersweet for Eva. There were pleasant flashbacks of innocence and purity, like memories of the beach. And there was photographic evidence of the better times, much like the image that stared back at Eva. But the happiness in those seven sets of eyes was all gone now—both physically and emotionally.

She remembered that terrible night. Just three weeks after Debbie's wedding, Norman came into the room she shared with Maria and shook her awake. "Eva, get up!" His voice was frantic. "Come on, get dressed!" She turned and saw his silhouette against the hallway light walking back to the doorway to turn on the bedroom light. A dull, yellow gleam from the bare 60-watt lightbulb on the ceiling coated the room in an instant. She propped herself up on her elbows and squinted in Norman's direction, as he aroused Maria from her own sleep. "What's wrong with you?" she groaned at him. "It's the middle of the night!"

"It's mom and dad," Norman said. "They got into some kinda car accident outside of Espanola. They're in the hospital in Sudbury. Edgar's outside in the car. Let's go!" A cold flash burst from her gut out to her fingers and toes. Her throat started to close. Bill had taken Clara to the bingo hall in Espanola that night, while he visited some buddies there. It started out so routinely, but then became so random and real—a nightmare she never had that was coming true.

All she remembered from the time gap between home and

the hospital more than an hour away was action. She didn't even remember what she was wearing. Maria couldn't find a sweater (it was a chilly mid-September night), so Eva grabbed a grey Sudbury Wolves hooded sweatshirt out of her own dresser. When she handed it to her, she noticed tears streaking down her little sister's face. She felt her own cheeks. They were wet, but she didn't remember crying then.

Urban commotion snapped Eva quickly out of that terrible recollection. From the street outside, a fire truck's siren blared suddenly and the engine's rumble shook the building. Melissa stirred and groaned behind Eva. "Man, it's too fuckin' loud here! Can't even get no sleep," she grumbled, in that thick rez accent that seemed to get louder only when the two young women were together. If there was one virtue to the mayhem of the city, Eva thought, it was there were always enough loud distractions to snap her out of any sad memories. "I need some smokes," Melissa proclaimed. "Wanna go to the store?"

"Sure," Eva replied. "I'm not getting anything done in here anyway." She wasn't sure how much time had passed since she got home from class, but she wasn't quite ready to get to work.

They got dressed and went back outside. They raced past all the open doors on their floor and the rest of the lingering residents in the foyer downstairs. Outside, the snow had let up and the clouds were clearing. It got colder as it got sunnier. Even so, the young women were jovial and warm with thoughts of returning home to their communities in just over a month.

They walked back out to Spadina and then south towards College. It was closer to suppertime and the workday was drawing to a close, so the downtown drones were packing street-cars and buses and walking in the opposite direction. It was like this every weekday. The core of the city seemed to exhale, letting an elephantine breath of exhausted souls back out into the suburbs.

"Can you imagine growing up here?" Eva asked. "Hell no!" Melissa replied. "Where do the kids around here even play?"

"Look at the people on that streetcar. They look so sad and tired."

"Yeah it's depressing man. Can't even go to bingo!"

They both erupted in loud, boisterous laughter and gave each other playful nudges. It was enough to alarm the handful of people in the two-metre radius around them, and most of them stared and/or scowled.

Stares were common. Eva and Melissa were an exotic mystery to a lot of the Toronto populace that sauntered past or saw them in shops or on the subway. When a stranger had time to give one of them a good look and ponder their background, it led to a lot of questions. *Look at her. Is she some kind of Asian? Latino? Maybe from Hawaii?* While there were tens of thousands of other Native people in Toronto, they were so spread out that the common city dweller probably would only see a handful on the streets in his or her lifetime. Even then, the contemporary living Native specimen would likely be someone panhandling, or down and out on a corner or in a park. Seeing someone from that background walking upright and seemingly "normal" was even foreign to people of wide multi-cultural backgrounds. The sad paradox was that this part of the land was a traditional hub for people like Eva and Melissa just a few short centuries prior. That history and those memories had all but been erased thanks to the authorities, and the new history being created here neglected or ignored the original people of the land. But one at a time, young students like these women from far away reserves were slowly infiltrating the psyche of the city.

Eva and Melissa got to their usual corner store in Chinatown, bought their smokes, and went back to their building.

The next morning Eva found herself in the class she disliked the most: Introduction to Canadian Politics. It was at 9AM every Thursday, and was usually more sparsely attended than any of her other courses, simply because it was an early-morning class late in the week. Eva noticed that students seemed more serious about classes earlier in the week. But this was crunch time. Finals were only about a month away, and term papers were due the week before that. So if there was a time to look like you cared about your grade, it was now, and there were more heads in the class than usual, albeit with bloodshot eyes and messy hair.

The auditorium was fairly silent as tired, book-weary and even hungover students shuffled in ahead of the instructor. It had a capacity of about two hundred and fifty people. It wasn't full when the semester started, and the numbers dwindled to roughly half that, a month in. If it wasn't a prerequisite for some of these students, they were likely to drop it. Here in the late 1980s, basic Canadian politics didn't really cater to the sensibilities of nineteen-year-olds who were there primarily for the frosh ride.

Eva took her usual spot about halfway up, all the way to the right side facing the front of the room; not quite tucked away, but not on display either. Still, she stood out in this crowd whether she liked it or not, being one of the few brown faces in the class and the only Native student, as far as she knew. She was outed early on in the semester when the first uncomfortable discussion of "Indians" came up, and the prof asked for a show of hands from the "Indians" enrolled in the course. Her arm slowly went up like a meek buoy in a placid yet adversarial lake. It essentially put a target on her back; not for the directed hostility of her classmates, but for an image to which they could attach all the stereotypes they learned growing up. And for the prof, a middle-aged, salt-and-pepper-haired white academic with a penchant for denim shirts, she became the poster child for the few things "Indian" that came up throughout the course. To him, she was a resource he could exploit to verify everything in the books from which he drew all his course material. Her people had no say in contributing to those books that would shape the ideas and attitudes of young Canadian academics. As such, she was called upon in every discussion. Most of the time, it was tedious and uncomfortable.

Eva slowly took her textbook and note binder out of her bag and placed them neatly in front of her. She kept her eyes down even after she opened the binder to a blank piece of blue-lined paper. She didn't have any friends in this class. She knew a few other students from residence, but they only shared cordial smiles upon locking eyes coming into the auditorium, and that's it. She was a lone warrior here in the fight for awareness, and it was hard not to feel vulnerable. It was a battle placed upon her shoulders by the dominant, non-Native academic world around her. And although she was still battling with a great deal of shyness, she was well beyond the initial reluctance and imposed shame, and carried herself with a newfound sense of pride and understanding.

She pulled a blue ballpoint pen out of a side pocket of her backpack and removed the blue cover and secured it on the end. She brought it up to the top right corner of the fresh page in front of her, and very legibly wrote "March 9, 1989" in very neat and symmetrical letters and numbers. There was still a constant, dim bustle hovering in the hall as students took their places. Suddenly, Martin the instructor, rushed in at his usual frantic pace.

"Good morning, everyone," he quipped with a faint hint of sarcasm, well aware of the lethargic atmosphere that hung in the large room. He was familiar with the common lackadaisical attitude at this time of the year among young adults like these. He wore tight acid-washed jeans, a yellow button-up shirt and yellow Wolverine shoes. Eva hadn't seen this getup before and chuckled to herself. "Please get settled. Today we're going to finish looking at the Constitution Act of 1982. As you know, this was basically our "Declaration of Independence" from Great Britain." His pace began to pick up, and he started a sharp line from one side of the front of the hall to the other, as he was wont to do. Eva wrote down "Constitution Act cont'd" at the top of the page.

"Today we're going to look a little deeper into the Charter of Rights and Freedoms," Martin continued. "Specifically, some of the fringe groups that benefited from this new law." Eva cringed. She knew what that meant. "We're talking about immigrants, Natives, and other people not necessarily at the forefront of building this country when the original British North America Act was signed back in 1867, essentially creating Canada."

Eva already felt a few of the quick glances from her classmates. She couldn't ignore them. At some point in this class, she would have to talk, whether she wanted to or not. Martin began his lecture. He picked up where he left off last week, painting former Prime Minister Pierre Elliott Trudeau as the mastermind and grand architect behind Canada's true "independence". "The greatest leader our country has ever seen," he carried on. He went on to explain how Trudeau "summoned" Britain's Queen Elizabeth II over to Canada to sign the Constitution Act into law. Essentially, the first part of that act became the Charter of Rights and Freedoms.

"This fortified a lot of the freedoms you enjoy today as Canadians," Martin continued. He explained how Trudeau had to win over provincial and political leaders while appeasing the legal community. Ultimately, Quebec didn't support the bill, "but that's a whole other can of worms we'll open later," he promised. One of the major accomplishments though, according to Martin, was Section 25. "This is how it reads," proclaimed Martin: "The guarantee in this Charter of certain rights and freedoms shall not be construed so as to abrogate or derogate from any Aboriginal, treaty or other rights or freedoms that pertain to the Aboriginal peoples of Canada including any rights or freedoms that have been recognized by the Royal Proclamation of October 7, 1763; and any rights or freedoms that now exist by way of land claims agreements or may be so acquired."

Eva expected this was where he was going. She took a deep breath, sat up straight in her chair, and glanced quickly around the room to see if any of her fair-skinned classmates were already scrutinizing her body language in the lead-up to getting called upon by their professor. To the left, a small set of eyes peeked in her direction under inflated blond bangs. There was no one to her right because she hugged the side of the auditorium. She was about to be put on the spot, and she knew it. Back in the Fall when classes began, she looked forward to these moments, despite her nerves. She anticipated this would be her time to shine; to be a true ambassador for her people and her community, and to engage in lively and enlightening discussions with like-minded, intelligent youth from other non-Native communities.

Eva was wrong. Instead, she found at best a general lack of awareness of the First Nations plight in Canada, and at worst, ignorance and veiled racism. A handful of students in some of her classes were sympathetic to the history and abuse her people endured. These few young people became her friends and allies. But that was only because they had some familiarity with Natives in the past that didn't fit the stereotypical bill of drunks or lazy losers. Most of the others had never met a Native person before—due either to their geographic or social upbringing—and they didn't care to learn. For some of these young people, Indians may as well have long been extinct in Canada. In these moments, instead of feeling like she was at the podium in a grand theatre of tolerance and understanding, she felt like she was on the witness stand, defending her people in the Grand Court of Canadian public opinion.

"Section 25 says that the rights in the Charter must not interfere with the rights of Native people," said Martin. "And this is where things get kinda iffy. Native people in Canada have special rights thanks to the treaties they signed with the Crown." He pushed his glasses up his nose and peered in Eva's direction. The hair stood up at the back of her neck and she felt blood rush into her face. She knew she'd be on the spot soon. The professor continued. "The Charter spells out clearly that other Canadians who don't have these rights can't argue that they've been treated unfairly."

He prefaced his targeting of Eva with an apologetic but seemingly insincere declaration. "Now it's no secret that Canadian Natives endured some real hardships while this country was developing. You can imagine that being displaced from the land you call home would take a serious toll. For Natives, it led to a lot of abuse and they're still getting over that." Eva cringed. He went on: "But fortunately they have some benefits thanks to the treaties that can help them get back on their feet. Eva, maybe you can remind us what some of those are?"

Eva's chest sank and she got a little dizzy. She was feeling more comfortable about engaging in class discussions than she was at the start of the school year, but being singled out like this was sometimes torturous. "What do you mean?" she asked.

"Well, with the treaty rights, what do those do to help a young woman such as yourself?"

She knew all eyes in the room were on her now. The brown, red, and yellow heads of hair in the rows in front of her were now craning their necks to look back at her. "Well, we can get funding through our bands for post-secondary education. That's really about it though," she replied.

"That's not exactly chump change though, is it?" Martin prodded.

"It covers our tuition and we get an allowance for living expenses."

A few minor gasps and utterances reverberated from the rows in front of and behind her. "Wow!" "Lucky." "That's not fair!" Eva tried to ignore those noises but it was just too hard. She was past the anxiety of being called upon, and now anger and frustration were starting to bubble up. She loved learning here, but she hated being the sole ambassador for the diverse and rich cultures across the country that were lumped together as "Native." She was the only Anishinaabe person many of her classmates would ever meet, so her example would likely shape their perceptions of Canada's first people for the rest of their lives.

"That's gotta help!" said Martin, with an air of condescension. Most of the instructors Eva met so far on this journey were very left leaning and sympathetic towards the First Nation cause. She suspected this one had some kind of agenda.

"You also don't have to pay taxes, right?" he pushed. "That's not really true," she shot back. "If we work on the reserve we don't pay income tax. Otherwise we have to pay just like everyone else."

"But you don't have to pay tax when you buy things at the store, do you?"

"Well, no. We're PST exempt," she said, explaining that showing a status card (or "Certificate of Indian Status", as it read on the pink laminated card) at the point of purchase means no added provincial sales tax. "But you can't use it everywhere. I stopped using it here in Toronto because stores either don't know about it or they don't want to go through the trouble of filling out the form and taking the tax off the bill."

"I find that hard to believe. We live in the most diverse city in the most tolerant country in the world."

"Well I find the attitude I get hard to tolerate when I try to exercise my right as a Native." She was getting fed up. She never spoke like this in class, but there had been a rage building within her for months. She felt like now was the time to put humility on the shelf.

"You can't deny, though Eva, that the rights your people are entitled to through the treaties give you a bit of a leg up on other Canadians." Everyone in the small auditorium was awake now and fixated on the increasingly tense discussion.

"A leg up? The treaties put us behind in the first place! We're still trying to catch up. Have you ever even been to a reserve before?"

"Yes, I've been to the Six Nations reserve."

"That's basically like a southern Ontario town. You want to see a 'leg up', up close and personal? Come to mine. You'll see the real Native experience—poverty and despair that shouldn't exist in Canada."

Her tone and vigour surprised even herself. Her label amongst classmates was evolving from semi-stoic wallflower to fervent troublemaker.

"Come on, Eva, get real." Martin dryly remarked. "It's been decades. It's time for Native people to move beyond falling back on the victim excuse." He moved to the podium and rested his elbow on the side. He lowered his chin and peered up at her over his glasses. Almost like a parent in the aftermath of a severe scolding.

"It's really time to get over it. Your peoples' rights were fortified by the law we're talking about today. Your communities have the tools. There's no reason your communities should be poor. There should be more of your peers in classes like this. The problems your people have are completely self-perpetuated."

At that moment the rage balloon within her popped. She inhaled deeply through her nostrils, and the anger exhaled out of her mouth as she deflated back to her normal self. This was a verbal ideological battle that she couldn't win with a louder voice. Everyone was staring at her now, but she wasn't nervous or anxious anymore. A sense of relief and pride overcame her. She would have to win over this stubborn and ignorant academic on paper, and she planned on doing that with her term essay and final exam. But this was enough for today.

"Fuck this," she muttered under her breath. She packed her bag quickly but suavely, grabbed her jacket, stepped calmly down the stairs and out of the auditorium.

"What are you doing here so early?" asked Melissa, in her deep, loud rez cadence. Eva was sitting at a table in the window of an on-campus coffee shop, reading over notes and picking at a bagel on a small white plate to the right of her binder. She looked up, unfazed by her friend's vociferous query. "I thought you had class right until noon?"

"I did," Eva replied.

"It's eleven. I thought I'd be here for a while until you showed up. How long you been here?"

"About an hour."

"Did you skip out of class? I heard you leave before I got up."

"I don't wanna talk about it."

"Alright then. I'm gonna get a coffee."

Melissa went up to the counter. The coffee shop was in a basement hall of the same building as the auditorium where her class was just wrapping up upstairs. Students sat at a few tables out in the hall, but Eva wanted to partially conceal herself in the enclosure of the actual cafe. The fluorescent lights overhead bounced harshly off the yellow-brown tile on the floor, illuminating the entire corridor with a dull, jaundiced wash. It was a sickly glow during the most stressful time of the school year, and it didn't help the unease in Eva's gut following the confrontation with her prof in front of her entire class. She noticed herself hunching over the table, so she sat up, pulled her tall, slender shoulders back, and tucked her black hair behind her ears. She realized she wasn't even looking at the notes in front of her, so she shut the blue binder and put it in her bag.

Melissa returned with a large triple-triple in one hand and a chocolate éclair in the other. She wore a dark blue hooded university sweatshirt over loose jeans, carrying her winter jacket under her arm and a backpack over the other. She planned on playing softball back home on the rez in the spring and throughout summer, and promised herself to get back in shape for that—but *after* enjoying indulgent treats like these in winter. She put her drink and treat down on the table and pulled the chair out across from her friend. She sat down with a sigh.

"Just a few more fuckin' economics classes," she proclaimed, speaking at conversation volume for her, which was much louder than anyone else's "inside voice". "This bullshit is gonna do me in!" If anyone else in the little café wasn't already looking at the women, they were now.

"*Shkinaa*!" Eva muttered between gritted teeth, stifling laughter. "Everyone can hear you!"

"Good, they should know that Economics class is bullshit too!"

They threw their heads back in laughter. Eva felt better now. Her friend brought her back down to earth just by being herself.

"Man, I had to put up with some bullshit myself in class today," Eva said, ready to vent. "Oh yeah, what happened?" asked Melissa, before chomping into the éclair.

"I basically had to be the National Chief again."

"Oh yeah, speaking for all Indians eh?"

"Yeah. The prof was going on about how we get all these freebies and how we need to get over the past. Typical shit."

Melissa shook her head in disapproval.

"I really didn't feel like putting up with it so I just told him off real quick and got outta there. They probably all think I'm gonna drop out now."

"Ah you'll be back so I wouldn't worry about it," said Melissa through a mouthful of French pastry and crème filling. Both young rez transplants were used to the general ignorance of their peers and instructors by this point, so once the dust settled after such confrontations in class, their resolve to finish their education grew even stronger.

Eva reached for her coffee, the paper cup weak and no longer warm to the touch. She brought it up to her lips to taste how cold it had become. It was tepid and bitter. She looked up, and over Melissa's shoulder she noticed a familiar fair face walking down the hall and towards the café. It was Lisa, another one of the girls who lived on their floor. Her tall, teased blond hair was like a beacon in the steady stream of heads bobbing through the mid-instruction shuffle. She spotted them and entered the café. "Here comes Lisa," groaned Eva under her breath.

"Hey ladies!" she chirped, stopping within centimetres of the table's edge. The high waist of her acid-washed jeans was at their sitting eye level, leading up to a loose white blouse and topped off with way too much makeup. "Whatcha doin'?"

"Hi Lisa," replied Eva. Melissa took another bite. "Just taking a break. You?"

"Done class for the week now! Heading back to rez soon. Hey what you guys doing tonight?"

"No plans really," shrugged Eva.

"I think a bunch of us from the floor are gonna head out to The Cavern later. You guys should come, I never see you out!"

Eva generally didn't like drinking or the bar scene, but after the morning she had, the proposition kind of intrigued her. "Yeah, maybe," she said. Melissa's eyes widened to the size of almonds. She liked to tie one on here and there, but Eva almost never partied.

"Come on, no maybes! School sucks right now. Blow off some steam!" Lisa insisted, her already shrill voice climbing.

"Yeah, okay. We'll be there." She smirked.

"Okay good! Come to my room for some drinks before we head out."

"Alright, thanks for the invitation."

"See you guys later!" Lisa turned swiftly and stepped out of the coffee shop.

Eva turned her attention back to her friend sitting across from her. Melissa's mouth was wide open with visible chunks of chewed pastry, crème and chocolate glaze on her tongue and lining her teeth. "YOU want to go out?" a bewildered Melissa questioned her friend.

"Yeah, why not?" replied Eva with a smile. "One last party before school really starts to get shitty."

"I'm shocked! You never want to go to that kind of place!"

"As if. It'll be fun!"

Melissa's surprise quickly became enthusiasm as she realized she wouldn't have to go to her cousin's to find someone to go out with. She usually went off-campus to party with some of the other Natives in the city whom she'd met through cousins, word of mouth, and the tiny yet connected urban Native community.

"Deadly, man! Well let's get outta here and go to the liquor store!"

Eva gulped back her cold coffee and Melissa took hers for the walk. They headed up to the LCBO on Bloor Street.

On the ground outside it was sunny and mild. Spring was looming, but the weather forecast was calling for one last cold snap into the weekend. The early tease of winter's demise seemed to have everyone on campus in good spirits. Eva and Melissa walked past smiling faces of all colours—students happy to have the week of classes almost over with. Some were ready to party, others planned to relax, and others still would get a jump on finishing those term projects.

All the fuss of schoolwork had been squeezed out of the conscious minds of the two young Ojibway ambassadors though. Melissa was excited that her friend was finally ready to party, prattling on about what they were going to get to drink, where they'd likely go later in the evening and who they may see. She was thinking about calling her cousin Wendy and her boyfriend Chuck—also from her home rez—to meet them at the bar later.

Eva's mind was elsewhere. She already had second thoughts about going out. She nodded in response to everything Melissa had to say, if only to appease her. Eva liked going out and socializing, but she didn't like to drink. She usually avoided going out because the pressure to drink was just too much. That pressure followed her from bush parties back on the rez here to the downtown Toronto university campus. There was the emotional toll too. She had seen too many lives ruined back home because of the bottle and she felt more comfortable avoiding it altogether.

She thought back to the first time she drank. She was fourteen, and her older cousin Nikki had just stolen a bottle of rum from her parents who were passed out. It was a Saturday afternoon and hangovers clouded the order in Birchbark. At sixteen, Nikki was already keen on drinking and smoking. The way she saw it, it was her duty to initiate her little cousin and prepare her for the teenage rites of passage that were almost inescapable on the rez.

There was supposed to be a bush party later that night. The plan was for Nikki to take Eva down to the beach and further down the shoreline. She'd give her a few shots of the rum to get her buzzed and used to the feeling. They'd go home to Nikki's and sleep it off, then head to the party later.

But Eva didn't make it. After a five shots, she puked and blacked out. Nikki took one arm over her shoulder and walked her back to her parents' house, sat her on the front steps, and took off. Eva remembered none of this. Her only recollection was of waking up with a pounding headache, dry mouth, and Clara's disappointed scowl staring her in the face. Her forehead wrinkled together and her eyebrows cut hard inwards. Her usual beaming smile was instead a sharp, sunken frown. Her thick lips were but thin pink lines seemingly glued shut. Her thick cheeks hung over the corners of her frown, as if to accentuate her disappointment.

Her mother's mouth looked the same way as she lay in her casket, albeit tighter to her face. These two memories were always entwined. Probably because they were traumatic and they both involved alcohol. It was impossible for Eva to shake one from the other.

Clara had actually won two hundred dollars at bingo that night in Espanola. She was elated when Bill picked her up. "We should come back down to Sudbury tomorrow and take the kids out for a nice supper!" she exclaimed. Bill agreed. They made their way out of town and stopped at the lights at the intersection of Highway 17. Bill waited for the green before turning left to head west back to the rez. A car was coming from that direction, but because the lights were changing, he was sure the other driver would stop. Bill himself was mildly distracted by his elation of the extra cash in his wife's purse. The oncoming car didn't stop, though, and slammed into Bill's side. A worker in the mine from Sudbury was behind the wheel. He was drunk. Emergency crews came. Cops took him away. Paramedics rushed Bill and Clara Gibson to Sudbury General Hospital. Bill died of internal bleeding on the way. Clara was suffering from the same injuries, but clung to life.

She died in the hospital before their kids arrived. All five were in the waiting room when the doctor delivered the news to Edgar. He asked him and Norman to go identify the bodies. The two eldest brothers came back with the grim news, and grief overwhelmed them. Edgar hugged each of his siblings silently and stoically, but unable to keep the tears from falling down his face. Norman stood in the corner and sobbed loudly with his face in his hands. Stanley hunched over on one of the waiting room benches, shielding his crying eyes from the obscene fluorescent yellow glow while heaving with emotion. Maria wept loudly into Eva's shoulder, while Eva wrapped her arms around her little sister, bulky in a two-sizes-too-big Sudbury Wolves sweater. Eva remembered smelling the sterile dryness of the waiting room and hospital hall. She refused to see her parents' bodies. The next time she saw their faces was at their funeral; her mother's mouth preserved in a stiff, thin frown, immortalized in Eva's memory for the rest of her life.

"So what do you wanna get? A twenty-sixer of vodka?" Again, the harsh mundanity of her current life snapped her back to reality. Melissa grabbed a clear bottle with a red and white label off the shelf. They were in the liquor store now.

"Uh ... I guess so. What can you mix that with?" replied Eva.

"Well, you can have it with orange juice or pop or just water, if you wanna be cheap. It's not as harsh as whisky or rum."

"Okay well let's get some orange juice. May as well be a little bit healthy eh?"

Eva tried to force the lame attempt at comedy to push her recent flashback as far away as possible.

"As if! You with the healthy talk! You're just skinny already!" shouted Melissa, looking her up and down. "It's okay to be bad once in a while."

Eva generally didn't like "bad" because it often led to trouble. But tonight she would make an exception. They split on the bottle and headed back to campus.

The blue cab pulled to a stop in front of the club called *The Cavern* on Bloor Street West. It was a usual venue in a string of consecutive nightlife locales for many of the students at the university. Thursday nights were for pubs and clubs, and Friday nights that boozy bar routine usually repeated. Saturdays were often reserved for house parties at campus fraternities or sororities. Eva and Melissa were largely unfamiliar with this routine, mostly because it cost a lot of money to party that much. They also didn't really fit in, nor did they want to, for the most part. But here they were, having fun with their non-Native counterparts on a night where having a good time transcended skin colour and social standing.

Eva was sitting in the back right and opened the door to step out of the cab. They had shared it with Lisa and her roommate, Julie. Eva heard the sharp crunch of the hard snow piled against the curb under her foot. It was much colder this evening than it was earlier in the day, and a light dusting of crystallized snow coated the hardening ice beneath. She exhaled as she stood up and a plume of moist breath shot high above the heads of the people standing in a short line by the front door. Melissa and Julia followed her, while Lisa paid the driver from the shotgun seat. "Ugh, I knew there'd be a bullshit line here!" grumbled Julie. The four shuffled to the back of the line to wait to get in.

Lisa reached into the pocket of her blue parka and pulled out a pack of cigarettes. She pushed it up from the bottom, opened the top flap and singled out three smokes from the left side. She handed two to Julie and Melissa and put one between her bright red-painted lips. She unzipped her parka to reveal a tight, white lycra shirt underneath, and reached into the inside pocket for her red lighter. Her heavily treated hair stood erect from her bangs, then spilled over her forehead like yellow willow leaves. She shielded it from the flame by holding it back with one hand while lighting her cigarette with the other, then passing it to the other girls.

"Thanks," said Melissa, lighting her own with a deep drag. She held in the smoke for a half-second then exhaled mightily into the late winter air. Similar clouds billowed from the other hopeful bar-goers in the line. A muffled, mid-tempo bass beat pulsed from within the club, and when the door opened to let people in and out, an indistinguishable sharp treble escaped with the warm inside air. "So what kinda music do they play here again?" she asked the others.

"Mostly stuff that's on the radio," answered Julie. "I usually only pay attention when I wanna go dance." Melissa nodded. She was used to some of the classic rock she heard growing up on her rez that seemed to carry over to the bars she preferred here in the city. She wasn't too concerned though, as long as they served more booze at this place to keep her buzz going, she figured she'd find a way to dance if she needed to.

"Can I just say again that I think it's totally cool how we're all hanging out?" proclaimed Lisa, more to the city street than to the other three. "I mean, me and Julie are so different from you guys, but we're all the same really. We're just people! We all want the same things …"

Eva and Melissa shared a quick, uneasy glance and offered an awkward smile in return to their white counterparts. They were all a little drunk, but Eva especially wasn't in the mood for that kind of exaggerated, intoxicated bonding. "Yep, we all want to love and be loved," she softly replied to the group in general.

Eva was feeling light-headed but in a generally good mood thanks to the alcohol. She never really felt the urge to go out and party like this, but it was a nice diversion from the intensity of the March crunch at university. She had all but forgotten about the heated exchange with her professor earlier that day. And although some of the ignorance she endured there carried over into their evening with these girls, she found it easier to tolerate. Questions like "so do you speak Indian?" and "can you build a tipi?" became more painless. The four of them sat around Lisa's room having some pre-club drinks before heading out, and despite the minor ignorance, Eva found it a rather pleasant bonding experience. Melissa enjoyed it too, but she was more enthused about the prospect of a different party scene.

Eva and Melissa learned a lot about their non-Native counterparts, and vice-versa. Lisa grew up in Guelph, and Julie in Windsor—southern Ontario cities that were much farther removed from Eva and Melissa's home communities. Although they were generally clueless about the Native plight in Canada, Eva made sure not to fault them. She believed that Lisa not knowing there were dozens of distinct Indigenous languages in Canada was due to the education system's shortcomings. But this evening wasn't about those frustrations. It was all about fun and making friends. Eva politely informed them that they were Ojibway, or more formally and politically correct, Anishinaabe, and their people spoke one of the dozens of different Native languages in Canada.

The line moved faster than they expected, and by the time they flicked their cigarette butts out into the snowy street, they were entering the club. The bouncer waved them through and they lined up at the booth to the right to pay the two-dollar cover charge. "Two bucks hooolay!" mumbled Melissa to Eva from behind her. "Ever, don't be so cheap!" Her tall friend replied. They giggled to themselves, knowing this kind of rez talk was as foreign as Turkish to most of the people in their immediate proximity. They paid, lined up again to check their coats, and walked down the hall to the main room.

It was a long, dark dance hall with a low ceiling. The bar was to the left of where they stood at the main door, and it opened up to a sunken dance floor on the right. High tables lined the outside, and a DJ was perched on the stage directly opposite the bar. Dark blue and purple lights flooded the room, with typical stage lights of orange, yellow, red, and green wavering randomly above the DJ. A thick haze of smoke hung about a metre above the fifty or so people writhing awkwardly on the dance floor to Paula Abdul's "Straight Up". The bass was especially loud and drowned out some parts of the vocal track of the hit song. No one moving on the dance floor seemed to mind though. "Let's get some drinks!" shouted Julie.

She led the group through the tightly packed crowd comprised of mostly white university students. They squeezed through small circles of bar-goers. Light blue and acid-washed denim was essential attire for both young men and young women, although it appeared dominant on the former, who wore it very tightly. Some of the men topped it off with button-down dress shirts of brighter colours, and others wore argyle sweaters or vests. There appeared to be only two hairstyles: either finely groomed or thick with a mullet. The women dressed slightly more diversely. Those who didn't don denim wore tight lycra skirts. Most of them wore loose-fitting blouses. And the hair was all big.

Julie pushed through and stuck her arm through a small opening at the bar between two big football-player types with varsity jackets. She smiled widely at one, who cleared a spot for her. Apparently her big brown eyes, elevated hair and unbuttoned-to-the-cleavage dress shirt won him over. She turned back to the group. "Whattya guys want?"

"Screwdriver!"

"A Blue."

"Yeah a Blue for me too."

Lisa turned to Eva and Melissa. "Wow, you guys really are tough northern broads eh?" she joked. Melissa shrugged. "Eh, I know what I'm getting, and I know the bartender won't be cheap on the booze," she answered. That seemed like a valid rationale to Eva, who really just wanted to begin this part of the night with something a little less extreme than hard liquor.

Julie passed back the drinks one by one, and led the way again as the four charged back through the boozy gauntlet of affluence and hormones. The Ojibway half of this assembled entourage wasn't as used to crowds like this, but the loud, obnoxious milieu around them was as exciting as it was uncomfortable. They held their drinks close to their chests as they powered towards the elevated outer edge of the dance floor. As packed as the bar was, they found a table for four against the railing. The glasses and bottles on the table were empty, so its prior inhabitants were either at the bar for another round or long gone. With no one left to guard the prime spot, it was fair game.

Lisa and Julie took the stools closest to the dance floor, across from each other, and Melissa and Eva nestled into the inside seats next to the constant stream of young people walking from the crowded tables to the bar, and back again. They seemed to fade into its darker shadows, Melissa wearing a long-sleeved navy blue Roots shirt, and Eva with a dark-green blouse tucked into her Levi's. The hair on their blonde and brunette counterparts was both lavish and ostentatious, compared to Eva and Melissa's; subdued, dark, sultry and mysterious. If anything, they stood out here.

The four young women sat for a few minutes and shouted over the loud music in an attempt to keep some sort of conversation going. They scoped out the guys on the dance floor and the ones that passed their table, occasionally making eye contact and smiling. Regardless of their very different backgrounds, this type of behaviour was universal, and with help from the alcohol, it brought them together on this rare and solitary evening. They giggled and huddled together to make the occasional lewd comment or joke. Melissa was on fire: "Look at that plaid shirt. He's built like a lumberjack! I wonder how good he is in the bush ... ehhhhh!" Eva felt herself occasionally blushing, but this type of talk wasn't below her. She just wasn't as crude as Melissa.

Salt n' Pepa's "Push It" bellowed over the sound system, and it was collectively agreed upon that it was time to dance. They tipped back the rest of their drinks, leaving two empty brown beer bottles and two lipstick-smeared clear plastic cups with ice on the table. Eva was the first to stand up so she led the way. It was a short walk from the table to the steps down to the dance floor. She didn't turn to see if the others were in tow. She felt all kinds of eyes on her as she began this brief jaunt, and she kind of liked it. Her beauty and poise were unparalleled in this bar this night. She was a tall, dark, and striking Ojibway woman unlike anyone in the young club-going crowd. She knew this brief boost of confidence was fuelled by the alcohol, but she didn't care. She cracked a slight smile and kept her gaze forward as she turned left and walked down the three steps to join the throngs writhing to the beat of the hit rap song.

Lisa, Julie, and Melissa followed and the four created a circle on the dance floor. There was no particular style or routine, they just moved along with the forty or so others with them. Dancing was secondary though. It was part of the whole modus operandi of catching someone's eye. They laughed and smiled at each other, before their eyes wandered to the young men around them and watching from the perch of the elevated table level. Some locked brief, inviting gazes, while others darted their eyes from dancer to dancer. Eva found the guys standing and watching a little creepy, so she turned her focus back to her friends. The music didn't stop, as the DJ churned out the hits. "Push It" bled right into Bobby Brown's "My Prerogative", and that segued seamlessly into Tone Loc's "Wild Thing".

The stripped-down drumbeat heaved the bodies forward. The piercing opening guitar riff was sharp and slightly unnerving, but its familiarity was reassuring. Above all, its sexual intimations harnessed the buoyant primal vigour floating in the room and brought it down to the dance floor. Many people in the club were there to get laid, and this was their cue to make their move.

The bi-racial group of four began to slowly drift from each other on the dance floor. Each stopped paying attention to the plight of the others, and they all spread out slightly. Melissa was the first to disappear. She went to the bar to get another beer. It was hot and they were all sweating, and she needed a break. Julie reconnected with one of the varsity jocks she had squeezed next to at the bar earlier. He had ditched his jacket, and was dancing awkwardly in a tight navy blue polo shirt tucked into his jeans. They smiled as they took turns shouting messages above the music into each other's ears. Just a couple of metres away, his friend had occupied Lisa's attention by complimenting her hair while rubbing his palm up the outside of her arm.

Eva, meanwhile, had locked eyes with an attractive tall guy dancing in the opposite corner. He was fair with finely curled hair that draped over the back of his neck. He stood out with his red Montreal Canadiens t-shirt that hugged his athletic build. He smiled, and started making his way over to Eva. His long, symmetrical face got closer and she was able to make out his bright blue eyes. A warming surge rushed through her body, signalling a hint of passion.

Neneh Cherry's "Buffalo Stance" started coming through the PA just as he reached her. They said nothing, only smiled and started moving to the music. A timeless practice done thousands of times a night in this city alone. This wasn't usually Eva's scene, but she knew what to do and felt comfortable after some opening jitters. They kept a close but safe distance, eyeing one another and smiling suggestively.

He was a few inches taller than Eva. She looked into his eyes, and down to his well-defined chest that was visible through the big blue "C" on his shirt. Further down he wore tight, light blue jeans that tucked into the tongues of his white, high-top running shoes. She didn't understand why city types insisted on wearing shoes like those on cold, snowy nights. Overall, though, she liked the whole package.

He was drawn to her exotic demeanour from across the floor. Her look was foreign to him. When he got closer he figured she was Indian. The long, black hair and beautifully well-defined slender face captivated him. Although she wore a slightly looser-fitting green button-up shirt, he could make out the outline of her well-defined arms. They circled each other as the song climaxed, and inched closer without ever touching. This mutual visual feast continued until there was a brief lull between songs. Finally, he leaned in. "Hi, I'm Mark," he shouted. Eva smiled. "I'm Eva. Nice to meet you!" They didn't speak again for one more song, when Mark asked her if she wanted to get a drink.

They stopped, and he moved his arms forward, motioning her to lead the way. She admired this quaint measure of chivalry and walked towards the steps up off the dance floor. The crowd had thinned out quite a bit. Her crew had only been there for about half an hour, but it was past midnight, and it appeared many of the young people who lined up to get into this dark, smoky club had either moved on to other bars or parties, or had gone home with new companions, or alone. Still, it meant easier access to the bar, and before long they were both leaning on it.

"What can I get ya?" he offered. Although they had only known each other for as long as a few pop songs and barely spoke a dozen words between them, she appreciated his kind manner and generosity. And above all, he was attractive. She worried getting another beer may not be "ladylike", so she simply responded "I'll have a rum n' Coke, please." He nodded, turned to the bartender and ordered. After paying, he took her drink and his beer in either hand, and said, "Let's go find a place to sit down."

He led the way this time, to the corner of the club farthest from the DJ and the dance floor. There was an upholstered bench that lined the wall with a couple making out on one end. Mark led Eva to the adjacent wall and motioned her to sit down. She glanced at the couple, and then up at him with an exaggerated look of disgust on her face before sitting down. "Get a room!" she muttered, loud enough for him to hear. He chuckled and they took their seats.

"So what brings you here tonight?" Mark asked. "Oh, some friends of mine from residence peer pressured me into coming out," she replied. "This is not usually my scene." She lifted the glass and tilted her head down to sip from the straw.

"Looks like they didn't have much arm-twisting to do!"

They both laughed. Eva noticed hers was much more pronounced, most likely because of the booze. That was followed by a brief moment of panic—she realized she hadn't seen Melissa, Julie, or Lisa since they were all on the dance floor earlier. She was snapped out of that by another question.

"Residence eh? So where do you go to school?"

"Oh, I'm at U of T, just down the road."

"What are you taking?"

"Just General Arts right now. I wanna eventually go to Law School."

"Cool. Good for you. There's probably not a lot of Indian lawyers eh?"

Eva didn't take well to general assumptions. She had already dealt with her fair share earlier in the day, and this was enough to snap her briefly into sobriety.

"How do you know that?" she snapped. "And how do you know I'm an Indian?"

Mark quickly sat up straight and fumbled his beer from one hand to the other. "Uh … I … uh … " he responded nervously. Mission accomplished, Eva thought. He was squirming. Her stone cold stare broke after just a few seconds. She didn't want to make this awkward for herself too. So she smiled and started laughing. "Relax," she said, "I'm just messing with you!" Relief swept his face back to life and he cracked a slight smirk too. "What about you? What program are you in?"

"Well …" he paused. "I'm sorta taking a break from school."

"Oh yeah? Christmas graduate?" she asked.

"I guess you could say that."

"So what do you do?"

"I work construction down by the waterfront. It sucks when it's this cold out!"

"I bet." Eva didn't pry further, but she was willing to give him the benefit of the doubt. He could be lying about having been a student, then quitting school to work. But just that morning she nearly quit being a student too, so she understood how hard that life could be. He looked young, so he must have been a student at some point, she thought.

They didn't notice someone approach until a shrill voice interrupted. "There you are!" remarked Lisa, eccentrically drawing out each monosyllabic word. "I've been looking all over for you!" She looked from Eva to the unfamiliar man beside her. "Hmmm, who's your friend Eva?" she suggestively prodded.

"Hey Lisa, this is Mark. Mark, this is Lisa, one of my friends I came here with."

"Nice to meet you Lisa," said Mark, as he stood up to shake her hand.

"The pleasure's mine!" she replied, as she reached out to grab his hand.

"Where's everyone else?" asked Eva.

"Julie's off in some corner with that football player. I was hanging out with his buddy but he's kind of a dud. I'm heading to the bar to get a drink to see if he gets more interesting."

"What about Melissa?"

"No idea. I'm sure she'll turn up."

Eva wasn't worried about her friend. She figured she may have left to meet some of her other friends at another bar. The Cavern was barely Eva's scene, so it definitely wasn't Melissa's. Melissa could hold her own on the streets of the Big Smoke, and Eva was sure she'd see her back in their room later.

"Well I'll leave you two. It was nice to meet you Mark!"

He smiled, and Eva lifted her arm to politely wave "see ya". They turned back to each other and she told him she was from the rez. He told her he was from a town in Quebec near Montreal, that she didn't quite catch. "I was wondering why you'd have the balls to wear a Habs t-shirt in Leaf country!" she proclaimed. They chuckled, and he inquired about her hockey fandom and she explained that up north, there wasn't much else to do. Toronto was the closest pro team so that's where her family's allegiances fell. Before long their drinks were done and he was up to get another round. Her head spun slightly, but she was confident she could keep it together. She trusted him and most of all, she trusted herself. Growing up on the rez hardened her to be prepared for the most random of situations.

Mark came back with new drinks and their conversation continued. It had progressed from the introductory to the mundane, but there was enough common ground to sustain an entertaining and flirtatious chat. He cracked lame jokes. She laughed beyond politely. He knew he was on thin ice, so he didn't ask Eva anything further about Native issues or culture. Suddenly

Eva realized she had sipped this rum n' coke a little too fast, and all the chatter started to blur together. She knew she was wasted, and she didn't like it. Mark was going on about something when she put her finger up to his mouth. "Shhhhh," she spat out. "I really don't feel good. I think I gotta go home."

His face went blank. "Are you okay?"

"I think I'm gonna puke," she slurred. "Where's Melissa?"

"What does she look like?"

"She's not here. Goddamn it!"

Mark looked around nervously. A thick haze of smoke still lingered in the air and limited visibility. "Maybe we should get you some fresh air," he suggested.

"I'm not leaving without her!" Eva shouted, before leaning forward to put her head in her hands.

"Come on," he said. "Let's just go outside."

He grabbed the clear plastic cup from her hand and set it on the small table in front of them. He downed the rest of his beer and put the empty bottle beside it. Then he carefully put an arm around her and held her left hand with the other, standing her up slowly. "Okay, watch your step," he reassured her, as he walked her past the bar towards the coat check.

"Where's your ticket?" he asked. Eva dug her hand slowly into the front pocket of her jeans and pulled out her coat check ticket. Mark put it together with his, handed it over to the blonde girl on the other side, and got their coats. His white leather jacket was much smaller than her parka, so he donned his before helping guide her arms through hers. They walked out the door into the now-frigid March night.

As she stepped onto the slippery sidewalk, the freezing air snapped Eva upright. Her head still spun and her stomach continued to turn sideways, but she was much more alert. She still needed Mark's help to walk. "Where are we going?" she asked.

"Just for a little walk," he tried to reassure her. "You need the air."

"Okay."

Eva clutched Mark's arm as they walked west along Bloor Street. She shuffled slowly, aware of the icy surface beneath.

Their breath shot ahead of them. It was close to minus ten degrees Celsius, and the slush from the day before was now rock hard. Eva didn't have the energy to speak, nor piece together where they were going. She was certain this was the way home. The walked for a few minutes westbound and the buzz of the strip began to slowly fade. Suddenly her stomach jumped. "I think I'm gonna puke!"

Thinking quickly, Mark ushered her into an alley to their left between a closed coffee shop and a laundromat. It was dark. She leaned over at the waist, expecting all the contents to rush out of her guts, heaving once, and then again, but nothing. She took a couple deep breaths, and slowly got her sober wits back. She sighed. "Whoa, that was close."

She looked around and noticed they were deep in the alley. Out on the street, the glow of the streetlights painted the fresh snow a cantaloupe orange. That was many steps away, and she didn't remember coming this far back. She looked to Mark and only saw that faint orange gleam off the left side of his face. Suddenly, she felt his wet, open mouth around hers as her back slammed into the wall. The force knocked the wind out of her and she couldn't breathe. She couldn't scream, and she struggled to put her arms between them as she felt him force his hand between her legs. Her heart raced and the panic returned. But this was a much more intense and frantic panic.

Instinct led her to bring her knee up sharply into his balls. It was harder than she had ever kicked anything before. He gasped and reeled backwards into the darkness. She turned to make a run for it, but slipped and stumbled on something. She couldn't tell if it was frozen snow or garbage. She fell to one knee, and before she could get back upright she felt a sharp tug at her hair. The force jerked her neck back violently. He stood her up to face him. She couldn't see his eyes, but she felt the rage cut through the cold and darkness.

"Fucking squaw!" he shouted, as he brought a heavy fist into her left cheek. She didn't see it coming, but she felt it. She fell to the ground, dazed. Her ears rung, and she couldn't make out anything else he was saying. That would be her last memory.

Mark delivered one final blow. He brought his foot back, and with all his force, kicked her in the face as she lay on the ground. She was out cold. He looked down and could barely make out her face in the orange light. Her hair concealed her eyes, and blood leaked from her nose and mouth. In a split second, fear gripped him and he dashed out of the alley.

Eva lay motionless on the frozen ground. The frigid night persisted, and her body temperature started to drop. Unable to awaken, her extremities eventually froze, and before long, her heart stopped.

STANLEY
Summer 1991

Stanley sat cross-legged on the dusty mound facing his sister's headstone. It was a simple, miniature grey monolith that stood about half a metre high. Tall blades of grass protruded from the base where it was nestled firmly into the ground. The grounds crew that came to cut the grass usually didn't bring their weed whackers too close to the grave markers for fear of knocking them over. As a result, the Birchbark Indian Reserve community cemetery was a finely manicured field of grass punctuated by stones and crosses that seemed to erupt from the ground with a green burst. There were also gravesites where the sod laid after the casket was buried didn't take to the soil. The grass ended up drying out in the eventual summer sun, leaving exposed dirt as a secondary marker for the final resting place of the community's deceased. That's what happened to Eva's.

She was buried in the late winter, and community workers came back in the early spring to lay the manufactured grass surface on top of the dirt. But for some reason the roots didn't penetrate the soil, and after the sod dried it still hadn't been replaced. Sitting there, the outsides of Stanley's bare lower calves became caked in a thick layer of light brown dust. His black running shoes were already coated in dirt from the walk there. He was unknowingly staring at his shoes, caught in a turbulent mental and emotional whirlpool of introspection. In two weeks, he would be leaving Birchbark to attend university in Ottawa. This would be one of his last visits with Eva for a while.

Stanley's eyes crept slowly but affectionately back up to the headstone. It read simply:

Eva May Gibson

October 13, 1969 - March 10, 1989

Blessed are the pure in heart, for they shall see God.

Matthew 5:8

It was a basic but fitting memorial, and it wasn't cheap. The surviving Gibsons would have never been able to afford it. Fortunately, the Birchbark band got money from Indian Affairs to pay for the burials of its community members, and that covered tombstones. As a result, most of the dead Ojibways received finely engraved markers of granite, marble, and sandstone, as if to leave them with a clean, elegant commemoration in death, regardless of how poorly they may have lived. The sad irony was that many community members got more money from the federal government when they died than when they were alive.

A dump truck rumbled by on the road behind him. The crackling gravel it kicked up and the roar of the diesel engine snapped him out of the momentary solitude. The cemetery was just off the main road through the community. A short driveway on the west side led to a big clearing in the bush about the size of a football field. It began only about a quarter of that size when the reserve was settled here about a century earlier. The Anishinaabeg needed a place to bury their dead, and it was far from their traditional burial grounds. The new settled graveyard expanded at an alarming rate in the generations that followed, due mostly to the sickness and tragedy that took so many people from their families and their community.

In the late spring and summer the cemetery was concealed by the lush green leaves of the birch, oak, and maple trees that served as a natural buffer between the living that traveled the road and the dead. But as the leaves fell late in the fall, and the winter eventually made everything grey, white and barren, the headstones and crosses that peppered the snow often became a grim reminder of the past. While many families tried hard to celebrate their dead and keep them in good memory, they were reminded every day how they died and why. It was nearly impossible to go anywhere on the rez without passing the final resting places of the loved and hated ones who had gone on to join the dead.

But this is where Stanley came for reassurance and guidance. He visited Eva regularly in the two and a half years since she was killed. He missed his sister dearly, and whenever he was walking by, he made sure to stop in, if just for a brief hello or to come and grieve privately. The visits were more frequent in the spring and summer when the weather was better and he was shielded by the green cover of vegetation, protected from the prying eyes of others in the community.

She was his hero. She summoned the courage to leave the

comfortable, natural confines of the reserve to try to chart a better future for herself, and for her family and her people by extension. He admired her resolve to come back and serve the community.

Just three years earlier Stanley and Eva sat together on the front steps of Edgar's house. The whole family just finished a going away supper for her. She was eighteen and ready to leave to start a new life in Toronto. And although she was only two years older than Stanley, to him she seemed like an immensely mature pioneer about to embark on a mysterious adventure. "Are you nervous?" Stanley asked. "Yeah," she replied, "pretty nervous."

"How come?"

"It's just so big and loud and crazy. And far away."

At that point Stanley had only been to Toronto once as a young child, and only remembered the annoying noises and strange-looking people. He also remembered that even though it was bright out, he couldn't see the sun in the middle of the day.

"But you gotta be kinda excited too, right?"

"Oh yeah. It won't be boring, that's for sure. A lot more to do than skipping rocks down by the water!"

They used to compete against each other skipping rocks from the North Shore. She taught him how to do it when he was five.

"Yeah but I heard if you even get close to the lake in Toronto all your hair will fall off and your skin will turn green. Good luck being a hotshot Indian lawyer after that!"

"Ehhhh, shut up!" She laughed, and poked him hard repeatedly in the side.

A crow perched high in one of the birch trees let out a sharp "caw" above the elevating buzzing of the crickets in the summer heat. The dry air was still, and carried the familiar rez sounds of barking dogs and roaring engines far and wide. In the distance, a pack of stray mutts chased a truck down the main road. The seasonal cacophony brought back focus. It was unusually hot for a day this late in August, and the sun baked the dark brown hair shielding his scalp. Sweat formed on his forehead and started to roll down his cheeks. His eyes behind his small rectangular glasses with black frames were dry. He was finished emotionally mourning his sister. His focus now was on honouring her memory by finishing what she started.

In the two-and-a-half years since Eva's death, none of Birchbark's youth left the community. Although there was only a handful of high school graduates (getting their diplomas from the school in the nearby town of Waverley), not one went on to pursue college or university, not even in Sudbury or the Soo. Her brutal beating in a dark back alley of Toronto sent a fervent chill through the rez that lingered. Parents and grandparents warned the youth about the potential dangers of the outside world, continually pointing to Eva's tragic example. No one said this to Stanley or any of her other siblings, but they sensed it. Eva became the poster child for everything that could go wrong beyond Birchbark's treaty-defined territorial boundaries. Yet another glum irony of rez life was that many of these young people endured cycles of abuse and other hardships while they stayed home in the community. It was a lose-lose situation.

But Stanley was determined to fulfill his sister's dream. He didn't even think twice about it when the time came for him to decide his path. He was always a slightly above-average student during his years at Waverley High School, pulling in a C+/B average while devoting a lot of time to sports. After grade twelve, though, he decided to take OAC classes in hopes of going to university and managed to get on the honour roll. As a quiet, shy teen in high school, he wasn't very social to begin with, and in his last year he put his meagre social life on the back burner to focus on his studies. Ultimately, that focus became leaving the rez. So he hit the books hard.

He excelled in the Arts in that final year of high school. An A was easy to come by in classes like English and History. He wasn't sure how that would translate into a career, and after vague, shallow advice from a brief visit with a high school guidance counsellor, he decided to apply to a political science program at the University of Ottawa. It was the same program his eldest brother Edgar tried for a semester many years before. It sounded familiar, and Edgar's failure to see it through didn't deter him. And this wasn't an attempt to show up his older brother and current family patriarch. Also, Ottawa seemed like less of an intense city than Toronto. Now, in just two weeks, Edgar would drive him there.

Stanley kissed his hand and touched the headstone. "I love you, sister," he spoke softly, as if to share this moment privately under the dodging eyes of the crows. He rose to one knee and stood up. He wiped his dusty hands on his cut-off jeans, and pulled his black Led Zeppelin t-shirt down straight. His cousin Presley got it for him at a store on Yonge Street in Toronto earlier in the summer. He picked up his backpack, slung it over his right shoulder, and turned to leave the cemetery. He walked out to the main road.

The primary vehicular artery through the community didn't have a name. Neither did any other of the roads that branched off it. There were no street signs on the rez. It was simply known as "the main road" or "the road". But according to the Ontario Ministry of Transportation's designation, and for map purposes, it was called "Birchbark Road". At least that's what the exit sign on Highway 17 said. It ran from the highway directly south to the North Shore, exactly eight-point-seven kilometres long. The official reserve boundary started about half a kilometre south of the highway, marked by a rectangular green sign posted on four by four wooden posts that read "Birchbark Indian Reserve".

The road was wide enough for two transport trucks driving by in opposite directions at a decent speed with some wiggle room. The surface was coated with grey gravel and its shape was slightly convex, with the edges sloping down into deep ditches on either side. Most of the time the slight trenches contained shallow standing water that often yielded countless mosquitoes. But because of the recent dry spell, the ground at the deepest points of the ditches was cracked and dusty, and the grass that lined the edges withered under a coat of grey dust kicked up from the road. It was easy to find all kinds of waste in these long crevasses, including fast food wrappers and brown beer bottles, their labels blistered, faded, and peeling under the intense summer sun.

Stanley was walking south, back into the heart of the community. He strode steadily on the left side of the gravel course, facing traffic. The road was mostly straight, so he could see who was coming from a kilometre away. The green station wagon off in the distance was his Auntie Kathy. He could hear dogs barking, and as she came closer he saw a trio of them chasing her car in futility. As she approached, she waved, but didn't slow down and kept going. She must be late for something, thought Stanley. Usually she stops to say hi. He smiled and waved back, as a cloud of dust enveloped him.

All of Birchbark's major buildings and landmarks were on the main road. The band office was the most northern of them. It was almost like a checkpoint for any non-Native visitors who happened to stray off the highway, looking for access to some of the north shore's beautiful golden and sienna beaches. Stanley was on his way home from the band office when he stopped at the graveyard. He had to pick up a package that the university sent (all Birchbark residents got their mail via general delivery to the band office). The big brown envelope contained orientation information about the residence he'd be living in for his first year. He browsed through the glossy material briefly on the walk back, but would go over it in more detail with Edgar later on.

Shorter dirt roads branched off from the main one, leading to the hundred or so homes that housed the roughly five hundred community members living on-reserve. The original Gibson residence was in the south end of the community. It was a far walk, but a valuable location. Stanley and all of his siblings spent a lot of time by the water year-round. Whether it was swimming in the summer or ice fishing in the winter, they were always there. Because of this heat, Stanley could only think of going for a swim. In the traditional Anishinaabe clan system, he was sure they were Fish Clan. He never heard his dad talk about that stuff though, and if he did know their clan, he took that information with him to the grave. He wanted to believe in the Spirit

World and his parents' eternal place there. It was but another void in his psyche and his identity.

A dark grey pickup truck full of young brown faces roared past him. "Stan the man!" someone shouted from the back. He recognized his cousin Presley's voice, but didn't see him. He was either in the cab or concealed in the back by the other young men. He only recognized a couple of the others from Birchbark, Danny Whitesky and Jared Wilson. The truck eventually slowed down and turned into the baseball field about a half a kilometre ahead on the left. It was directly across from the elementary school on the other side of the road. Stanley figured he'd see what they were up to.

The baseball field was in a clearing in the bush, much like the cemetery. It lay slightly lower than the main road itself, having been a swamp centuries earlier. The outfield fence was built against a beautiful backdrop of birch and oak trees. When Stanley stepped down from the road, he could see the other young men unloading bats and bags of gear from the truck. There were only seven of them altogether—hardly enough to field even one team for a game. This was likely just a casual round of Five-Hundred Up to kill some time. "Hey buddaaaayyy!" shouted Presley, as he saw Stanley walking closer. The cousins were the same age, but Presley was much more outgoing. Still, they were close and the bond of family transcended simple friendship.

"What's going on, shithead?" quipped Stanley as he reached the truck. "Fuck all, just gonna hit the ball around," replied Presley. "Some of Danny's cousins are here for the weekend from Stoney," Stoney Inlet was another Ojibway reserve farther south, on the other side of Sudbury. Danny led the introductions— Chris, Chucky, Frank, and Victor. Although Stanley wouldn't remember their names, he shared the traditional "nish" handshake with each of them. It was a grip common among Native men—locking the thumbs in an upward position, instead of gripping the fingers palm-to-palm. The boys ranged in age from sixteen to nineteen, and were all a deep shade of bronze after months in the summer sun. They wore variations of shorts, t-shirts, ballcaps, and high-tops.

"Wanna play? I got an extra glove," said Presley. He and Stanley were roughly the same height, but Presley looked like more of an athlete, with a lean build and muscular arms and legs. His backwards green Oakland Athletics hat kept his shaggy black hair out of his eyes.

"Nah, I gotta get home and talk to Edgar about school stuff," replied Stanley. "I just had to pick up some mail from the band office and he wants to see it right away."

"So you're really selling us out eh?" Presley chuckled, only half-joking.

"Oh fuck off. I'll be back, geez."

"Heh heh yeah I know cuz, I'm just busting your balls," Presley had dropped out of high school the previous fall, but vowed to return for the upcoming fall semester.

"I kinda wanna just get it over with," said Stanley. "This shit is really stressful."

"Ah you'll be alright cuz. We're proud of you. Just don't forget about us little people back on the rez!"

A smile crept up from the corner of Stanley's mouth. The sentimentality ended there though, as Presley gave him a friendly shot to the gut, then rustled his hair.

"What are you doing tonight? I think there's going to be a party at Tina's."

"No plans."

"Alright swing by there later. I'll have some beers for ya."

"Alright, cool," Stanley wasn't much of a drinker to begin with, and he rarely did after Eva died, but he knew deep down he couldn't turn down his cousin's gesture. "I better get home. See ya after!"

"Later!" The rest of the crew flashed peace signs as Stanley turned to walk off. Presley climbed into the cab of Chris' truck to turn up the tape deck. The song was "Welcome to the Terrordome" by Public Enemy. "Alright, I'm hitting first!" yelled Presley, as the rest of the young men ran into the outfield. Stanley looked over his shoulder one more time and smiled.

He faced the school as he walked back up to the road. The single-level, four classroom building with a modest gymnasium had a yearly enrolment of about fifty kids on average, from kindergarten up to grade six. The red brick walls led up to sheet metal roofing that was painted brown. It was built just seven years earlier so it was still relatively new, and had yet to show any real signs of wear. Stanley himself never went to school here. Back then, kids in Birchbark only did kindergarten in the community, in a one-room school house next to the old band office. After that, they were bussed a half hour away to finish their primary and secondary education in Waverley, the town of about five thousand people farther west on the highway.

But early in the 1980s the community's Chief and Council decided they wanted more autonomy over the education of the community's children, and rallied the federal government for funding to build a bigger school to teach more children on-reserve. They succeeded, and while it was still a work-in-progress, more and more kids became engaged in education simply because they could access it closer to home. There was still a lot of work to do to incorporate a more Anishinaabe approach to education (as most people in the community were still re-learning the old ways). And beyond grade six, kids still had to go into Waverley, but the initiative was new enough that people remained hopeful it could help chart a new course for the community's future.

Stanley never got to take advantage of the new school because he was already going into grade seven in Waverley when it opened. His younger sister Maria, however, was going into grade six, and their parents happily took her out of the town school and enrolled her on the rez for just that one year. In the end, though, it made little difference to Stanley because he was dedicated to getting his education, thanks largely to the influence and guidance of his older sister Eva and her studious nature.

Back on the road, he was heading south once again towards home. The sky opened a little wider, closer to the north shore of Lake Huron. The north end of the community was defined by tall deciduous and evergreen trees that hung over the roads and scattered homes nestled within the thick forest. These naturally random wooden pillars were blanketed at the base by dense shrubs. The vegetative shelter was both calming and forbidding by day, and eerie by night. As he journeyed through the lush foliage, he entered the more spacious territory of the shoreline. More of an actual village existed closer to the water, with houses placed within a neighbourly vicinity of one another on a loose grid of dirt roads. A couple other community landmarks stood amongst this loose concentration of rez development, including the water treatment plant and the community hall.

Stanley took a left, stepping off of the main road. His parents' home was one of only two on a short driveway of grey, compacted dirt. The other housed Jimmy King and his family. As his time to leave drew closer, each familiar walk home garnered a little more emotion and sentimentality. This time he felt a lump in his throat and moisture in his eyes. Maybe it was the visit with Eva. Maybe it was seeing his cousin and his buddies carrying on as rez kids do. Maybe it was the awkwardness of having to talk with Edgar about trying to succeed where he failed. Either way, he choked it back and shook it off as he approached the wooden steps to the aging spruce-needle green painted house. The colourful coat on the outside chipped and flaked off, almost as if the exhaustion of the emotional turmoil this home had endured was wearing on it.

The creamy yellow fluorescence of the overhead lights and the sterile dryness of the hospital waiting room were unforgettable. He sat hunched over, staring at the criss-crossed thin emerald lines that patterned the vinyl flooring of the waiting room. His sisters sobbed together. Then his brothers came in. One was nearing hysterics. He knew at that moment his family was going to fall apart. His eldest brother came around and sat down beside him. "We'll get through this, bud, I promise," he spoke softly as he wrapped his right arm around his shoulder. Stanley remembered being tense and unable to relax. The muscles between his shoulder blades hurt as his torso constricted, as if a black serpent of grief squeezed the hope and happiness out of his adolescent spirit. His parents were dead.

The basement of Bill and Clara Gibson's house was high above the ground, so eight wooden steps led up to the porch at the front door. Stanley bounded up in four quick leaps, two steps at a time as usual. He opened the screen door—the heavy wooden main door was open, signalling someone home—and stepped inside. He looked across the kitchen and saw Edgar lying on the couch, reading. "Aanii, brother," he muttered from under the book. "Hey," Stanley said back, looking down at his shoes as he stepped on each heel to take them off.

All five Gibson children grew up in this house. Before their parents died, it was just the three youngest living there. Edgar had his own one-bedroom apartment in Birchbark's only housing complex. He moved back in with the family for a few months after dropping out of university, but didn't feel right living off of his parents so he found work and moved out, "like an adult", he said. At the time Norman was bouncing between places in Sudbury, working odd jobs in construction. He was home visiting the night they died.

Edgar moved back in after Bill and Clara's accident. He took it upon himself to raise his younger siblings in the absence of their parents. At the time, Eva, Stanley, and Maria were sixteen, fourteen, and thirteen years old respectively. His girlfriend Alana moved in shortly after Eva left for school, and a little more than a year after she died Alana gave birth to their first son, Dylan. He just turned a year old earlier in the summer. Youngest sister Maria had her own room in the basement. So as always, it was a home full of life, only now the spectre of death continually loomed in each room.

Stanley stepped through the modest kitchen into the living room. The two common areas opened into each other, and without any sort of divider they were essentially the same room. It's where everyone did their eating and socializing, and although it was small and cramped at times, it was easy just to move from the kitchen table to the living room after a big meal. He sat on the faded brown upholstered chair across from the sunken dark green couch that Edgar was sprawled across. He set his backpack down on the floor beside him.

Edgar lay his book down on his chest. It was the most recent in Stephen King's *The Dark Tower* series. The paperback was sprawled open about halfway across the American Indian Movement logo on his black t-shirt. He cut the sleeves off at the start of the summer, as he did with most of his shirts. His long, coarse, dark hair draped across the cushion and the arm of the couch. It didn't look good loose so he usually kept it tied back. He looked up at his little brother. "So, what did they have for you?" he asked, knowing that Stanley got a call from the band office about mail.

"It's another package from the university. I only opened it quickly to see. Looks like stuff for the residence building."

"Oh yeah, right on. Bring it over here then."

"Where's Alana and Dylan?"

"Went into town to get some groceries."

Edgar sat upright on the couch as Stanley pulled the package out of his bag and went over to join him. He sat down and opened the glossy folder.

"Looks like they got a new printer," Edgar joked, having received a similar package years before. Stanley scanned introductory blurbs with headings like "President's Message" and "Life On-Campus". Each of the colourful pages was illustrated by pictures of mostly-white students, purposely diversified by the carefully-placed occasional Asian guy or black girl. "Looks like they've done a lot more recruiting since I was there," noted Edgar, sarcastically. Stanley smiled nervously, knowing that loneliness was a real possibility when he stepped into the wider, scarier "white" world. Out of all the other unknowns and variables attached to going away to school, being the only Indian kid in his classes and social circles is what worried him the most. He knew Eva struggled with that. But at the same time, it motivated her to push forward and succeed. Stanley vowed to carry himself with the same pride and resolve.

Stanley pulled out a few more sheets and the brothers looked at the residence building floor plan and studied the rooms. They were typically laid out in rows of two-bed shared living quarters with bathrooms and shared common rooms at intervals. Stanley wouldn't find out until he got there who his roommate would be.

"Shared rooms still eh," noted Edgar.

"Yeah."

"Looks like you'll have to go into stealth mode when you jerk it now! Hahahah!"

"Shut up!" Stanley shoved his brother in the side with his forearm. "I'll have ladies to do it for me."

"You wish. But if you're lucky you might find a couple that love Indians. All that new age shit that's coming back might work in your favour. Hippy chicks might be all over you. You better start growing your hair now!"

"Was it like that when you were there?" Stanley was a little apprehensive asking his brother about his short stint at the University of Ottawa.

"Nah, when I was there it was all Duran Duran and the Thompson Twins. People were all about image and taking hours to make sure they looked good for class. A guy from the rez doesn't fit in with that crowd."

"I'm kinda worried about that."

"Ah don't worry too much Stan. Everything that's old is new again. I've noticed people your age discovering Led Zeppelin and Pink Floyd. Look at your shirt! Soon it'll be Neil Young and Joni Mitchell and all those old hippies. And you know who was one of the most popular hippies of all?"

"Who?"

"Buffy Sainte-Marie. One of the most famous Indians ever. Once your new friends there catch wind of her, you'll be more than just a cigar store Indian in the dorm hall. Just be careful with your wood!"

They both laughed.

The truth was a lot had changed since Edgar himself tried university back in the mid-1980s. Back then, Native people were still anonymous mysteries that lingered in the footnotes of the rapidly evolving story of Canadian society. They were generic brown faces wallowing in the periphery of the national cultural scope; mere specks of faded wool on the fraying fringe of the social fabric.

People Edgar met during his time in the city didn't even know that there were different kinds of Indians. They were unaware of the different language groups and cultures that once thrived just within walking distance of the city of Ottawa. The city itself was erected upon un-ceded Algonquin territory, and eventually became the symbolic and legal metropolis of colonialism in the northern half of Turtle Island—or what non-Natives called North America.

Edgar's classmates and peers in the city were generally as equally clueless about culture as they were about history. "Treaties" were a foreign concept to anyone who bothered to engage him in discussions on his background. And the idea of the Indian Act was just too preposterous to be an actual Canadian Law, with its seemingly far-fetched clauses forbidding traditional dancing, ceremony, and language. "There's no way that actually happened in Canada," one young counterpart once told him. "We celebrate culture here."

The ignorance that confronted Edgar was frustrating, but the stereotypes were unbearable. If the image of the good, noble, honest Indian was dead, the lazy, drunk, criminal was alive and well in the minds of other Canadians. That's what he learned in his brief stint off the rez, anyway. The few Natives that he did see in the city were homeless, panhandling on Rideau or Elgin streets. If this was just a thumbnail sketch of the urban native experience in his mind, it was a dark and finely-detailed two-storey-high mural in the minds of everyone else.

Others expected Edgar to be a drunk, so he became one. At first he drank alcohol socially to fit in; to be invited along to house parties and to be friendly during pub nights. He found that the uncomfortable discussions about his background were less likely to come up in those situations, likely due to the dumbing-down the whole booze and party process had on him and his peers. If anyone did have questions and comments, being drunk made them easier for him to handle or to simply brush off. And really, it was fun going out and partying. It was easy to talk to girls and he made a few buddies along the way.

But it wasn't emotionally or financially sustainable. Edgar found himself drinking more and more during the week, and going to class less and less. He was already limping through the whole Indian-student-in-the-city ordeal, and the harder it became to figuratively walk this new path, the more of a crutch alcohol became. He had no friends outside of drinking circles, and he failed to really connect with the few other Natives he came across in Ottawa. When it was time to go home to visit for Christmas, he packed as much as he could, knowing he may not return. He didn't.

This was the fate he wanted his little brother to avoid. And he was confident that Stanley would. His little sister Eva made it beyond Christmas and was well on her way to getting her education. But that was stolen from her. He had to distract himself from those thoughts whenever they crept back in. They would sneak up behind him like prowling black snakes, and attack once he let his emotional guard down.

"Never mind the university, are there a lot of 'Nishnaabs in Ottawa anyways?" Stanley asked.

"Yeah, but they're hard to find," said Edgar.

"How come?"

"Well, they're pretty spread out right across the city. There's no Chinatown for Indians."

"How do you find them?"

"Well, there's the Friendship Centre. They always have stuff going on like socials and bingo and that kind of thing. I didn't go there as much as I should have though."

"Sorry for all the questions man. Honestly, I'm just getting kinda nervous."

"Don't sweat it little bro, you'll be fine. Just don't booze too much."

"Eh, I don't really like boozing anymore anyway."

"Good."

"Are there a lot of Ojibs over there?"

"Yeah, some, but that's Algonquin territory. Lots of Mohawks there too. But I think you'll see a lot more Indians of all types move there in the next few years. Things have changed quite a bit lately and I think the government needs to hire some to sort shit out."

It had only been a year since the infamous and historic Oka Crisis of 1990. A group of Mohawks in Quebec were fed up with having their land encroached upon by non-Native forces for hundreds of years, and it boiled over when developers made plans to build a golf course overtop a traditional burial ground. The Mohawks occupied the area and a high-profile dispute dragged on for months. It became violent, with one Quebec police officer shot to death and a number of community members nearly fatally-injured. The dispute made national headlines and put wider Native issues into the spotlight. Images from the blockades at Oka and from support rallies and marches in towns, cities, and reserves flickered across TV screens from east to west. For people like Edgar and Stanley and their friends and relatives in the community, it was a unifying moment of resistance.

So much so, that Edgar, Norman and their cousin Jay (Presley's older brother) made the nine-hour drive from Birchbark to Kanesatake in Jay's black Dodge Ram to help the Mohawk Warriors where they could. They didn't join them on the front lines of the blockade or in the Pines (ground zero for the community members reclaiming the traditional space), but they helped with organizing and delivering supplies where needed. They also shuttled the warriors and their supporters between strategic points.

They were there for four days before Norman got into a shouting match with a non-Native town resident outside a grocery store. They traded barbs back and forth in English and in French—likely not understanding each other at all—before they came to blows. Norman beat the man so badly that he had to be hospitalized, and word quickly came back to them that the *Sûreté Du Québec* had a warrant out for Norman's arrest. He, Edgar and Jay got in the truck without hesitating and drove through the night back to Birchbark. None of them ever returned to Quebec.

"The government's doing all kinds of studies and reports

on Indians now," explained Edgar. "I think they realized they fucked up pretty bad with us over the years. Oka was a pretty big turning point."

Stanley remembered very vividly. Everyone did. There was even a big rally in Sudbury with people from all the reserves within an hour's drive of the city. "So you think that'll make things better?" asked the younger brother. "People were saying some pretty nasty stuff last year."

"Eventually, yeah. Just don't let all that stuff get you down. I let it do me in back then. I still regret it."

"Alright. Miigwech bro. I'm gonna go put this stuff with the other big pile of paper they sent me."

"Those white people have no respect for the trees!"

"Murderers!"

Stanley clenched his fist and shook it, gritting his teeth through a sarcastic smile at his brother. He got up and went down the hall to his room.

Stanley was sitting in his Grade 11 English class when there was a knock at the door. His teacher, Mr. Bennett, got up to answer it. It was Waverley High School's principal, Mr. Adamson. "I'm here for Mr. Gibson," he said. He took a step into the class and saw Stanley in his usual seat near the back. "Stanley, can you come with me please?"

The principal's sombre demeanour caught Stanley off-guard. "You better bring your stuff," he said. Stanley shoved his binder of notes and his tattered copy of *Brave New World* into his backpack. The whole class was eerily silent as he got up to leave. When he reached the front of the class, Mr. Adamson put his hand on his shoulder and led him out. The contact was strange and oddly comforting at the same time.

Edgar was standing in the hall. He was looking down at his boots, the snow melting into puddles around them. He looked up when he heard the door close as Stanley and the principal came out into the hallway. "I'm so sorry Stanley," Mr. Adamson whispered as he squeezed Stanley's shoulder one last time. Confused, Stanley looked at his brother. Edgar's face was pale and sunken under the bright overhead lights of the high school hallway. His bottom lip quivered. "Grab your jacket from your locker," he said. "Let's go home."

Stanley followed his brother's order and once he closed the metal locker door and shut the combination lock, he and Edgar walked down the hall and out the front door. They turned right, heading for the parking lot. The snow was coming down heavily and packing a thick, wet, late-winter white layer on the sidewalk. Stanley gripped the strap of his backpack tight over his right shoulder and curled his other hand into a fist in his jacket pocket. His palms were sweating and his ears were ringing. His brother's emotionally broken face indicated something was terribly wrong.

They approached Edgar's blue station wagon and slowly climbed in either side, leaving wide footprints from their winter boots in the snow. Edgar's appeared to drag into each other at closer intervals, leaving a melancholic, reflective track, while Stanley's showed much longer strides in a bout of uncertain anxiety. As he shoved his backpack to the floor and shut the door to his side, Stanley hurriedly fastened his seatbelt. His hands were shaking. He looked left at his brother, who was staring into the steering wheel. It was a half an hour's drive back to Birchbark. Edgar knew he couldn't leave his brother on edge that long. He had to tell him, right here in the high school parking lot.

"It's your sister ... Eva ... " he started, before his voice faltered and collapsed. He cleared his throat.

"She was found dead this morning in Toronto."

The pickup truck rolled slowly into the driveway of Tina King's house, pulling in behind a dark minivan. It was dusk, but the floodlight on the front porch shone brightly into the front yard, illuminating the six other visiting vehicles there for the party. A few stragglers stood out front, smoking cigarettes and holding bottles of beer. Once Chris shut off the engine, they could hear the bulk of the activity coming from the backyard and from inside the house—yelling, laughing, and the bass from the stereo. Presley turned to Stanley where they sat in the back of the truck. "Looks like it's party time!" he said, before slapping him on the thigh.

Jared grabbed one case of beer from the cargo floor, and Presley and Stanley grabbed the other two. The glass bottles inside clinked sharply in unison, almost harmoniously foreshadowing the false euphoric joy inspired by the liquid within. The three of them jumped out of the back with Danny and Victor, while Chris, Chucky, and Frank piled out of the cab. There were eight of them altogether. Stanley didn't plan on drinking, so they had seventy-two bottles of beer to split between seven teens. They worried they didn't have enough.

They strolled coolly up to the house, a teenage 'Nish entourage decked out mostly in hooded sweatshirts, shorts, running shoes, and ball caps. They appeared homogenous, but each had his unique share of struggles and reasons for drinking (or not drinking) tonight. For some of them it was learned behaviour. For others it was a numbing distraction. And for even just a couple of them, it was simply juvenile fun.

They were all aware of the stereotypes associated with Native people and alcohol abuse, but for the most part they tried to ignore them or didn't care. A teenage drinking party on the rez is the last place where anyone would judge them for that. They'd find judgment in other personal traits or details of each other's backgrounds, but that would happen much later into the night, and would definitely lead to physical altercations. At a party like this, there would be blood. That was always a given.

That's what turned off Stanley the most about the whole rez party scene. It always started off jovially. But at the drop of a hat it could get ugly. If it didn't happen sooner, it would always happen later. Being the one who usually didn't drink, it was always up to him to break up fights, calm indignant party-goers, or call the cops. The few times he did indulge in booze himself was to try to avoid that responsibility or to ignore some of the emotional hassles that he and everyone else brought with them to the party. Everyone was potentially a walking time bomb, including himself.

Jared and Danny led the way, while Stanley lagged in the middle of the pack with the rest of the boys. Coming from another reserve, they were by and large foreigners, and would likely be sized up immediately by intrigued female eyes and wary male ones. They walked into the yellow glare of the floodlight, which spilled out in a parabolic radiance onto the brown siding of the house and onto the gravel of the driveway. Standing under it were Kelly Whitesky and Ashley King, smoking cigarettes and holding bottles of beer. They wore the female equivalent of the rez outfit—baggy t-shirts over fringed jean shorts with colourful high-top sneakers. Kelly's hair was cut in a short, black, bob, while Ashley's was long, wavy, and brown. "Hey cousin," Kelly said to Danny, before blowing smoke out of the side of her mouth. "You boys gonna stay out of trouble tonight?"

"Nope," he replied. They were the same age. "Unless you guys start giving us shit!"

"Who are your friends?" Ashley asked, smirking and eyeing each of them intently. They put down their cases of beer and Danny introduced his cousins and their friends. For the girls at the party, this was fresh blood: young men new to their community who they likely weren't related to. Dating on the reserve was always a frustrating dance of developing a crush, initiating the chase, but then stalling it to inquire with an aunt, uncle, or grandparent whether you were related to this potential new mate. Most of the time it ended in disappointment or mild frustration once a young romantic learned the object of their desire was, in fact, a cousin. So anyone from outside of the community was an exciting new prospect. Chris, Chucky, Frank and Victor would be the hits of the party among the girls, but the instant adversaries of the boys. Fights were a certainty, tonight.

"Oh hey Stanley!" said Kelly as he got to them. "How's it going?"

"Pretty good thanks," he replied shyly, looking down at his still-dusty black sneakers. Kelly was one of his first crushes as a boy. He was thrilled to find out back then that they weren't related. Sadly, the crush was never reciprocated.

"You're going away to school soon eh?"

"Yeah, not next weekend but the weekend after."

"Are you excited?"

"Yeah I guess so. I'm gonna miss everyone here though."

"Ah, we'll always be here. You're doing a good thing though. We're proud of you!" She raised her arm and squeezed his shoulder. The contact gave him goosebumps.

"Miigwech Kelly," he smiled. "I'll be back all the time."

"I know, the rez always sucks everyone back in!" She laughed. He responded with nervous laughter.

"Well we should celebrate," she added. "Want a beer?"

"Nah not right now. Thanks though. Maybe later."

"Okay. That's why you're able to get outta here Stanley. You're one of the good ones."

He didn't know how to respond to that so he just smiled. "Here, I better get a hug from you now before we don't have a chance," she said, breaking the brief, comfortable silence. With her burning cigarette still in her right hand, she carefully wrapped her arm around him, with her left hand still dangling by her hip holding a half-empty beer. He responded in kind, mindful of the smoke. It was a comforting beginning to what would likely be an uneasy and unpredictable night.

Jared, Chris, and Frank picked up the cases and led the way around the left side of the house. The five others followed to join the party. The music got louder as they came around the corner to the back yard. The stereo speakers were propped up on the railing of the wooden deck to the right, blasting AC/DC's "Moneytalks" over the football field-sized lawn bordered by silhouettes of indistinguishable trees. About three dozen people were scattered about the yard, mostly concentrated around the raging bonfire in the middle. There was another floodlight in the back, and its yellow shine both battled and blended with the orange of the fire to illuminate the young brown faces.

They found a spot on the periphery of the circle surrounding the fire, and put down the boxes of beer. This would be their post for most of the night. They had too much beer just to cart around at will, so someone would have to stand by to watch it. Although there was an abundance of alcohol at the party, it wasn't exactly easy to come by. Underage kids would have to pay an older relative or friend to go into town to buy it for them. Most of them didn't work, so they didn't have a lot of money to begin with. So as the bottles empty as any party goes on, the remaining alcohol becomes a hot commodity in a self-destructive market of despair and dependency. The brown bottle is the holy grail for a drunk, desperate teen thief.

Frank ripped open the cardboard top of one of the cases and started handing out beer. As he leaned over, he held a bottle in the air for the next person to take. Presley grabbed one and twisted off the cap. So did Danny, then Jared, then Chucky, and so on. Within seconds they were all standing in another smaller circle, their right arms cocked at a ninety degree angle at the elbow just above the waist, fingers wrapped around the warm bottles.

By Frank's count eight of them were drinking, so by the time he counted eight bottles he'd pulled from the case, he stood up. He surveyed the circle to see who still needed one. Stanley stood across from him with his thumbs in the pockets of his jean shorts. Frank pointed the butt of the bottle in Stanley's direction and nodded. Stanley pressed his lips tightly together in a quarter-smile, shook his head, and showed the palm of his hand in the non-verbal "no thanks, I'm good." Frank shrugged and held on to the beer for himself, knowing he'd need another in mere minutes. He shoved it under his arm briefly to twist the cap off the one he pulled for himself. "Stan usually don't drink at these things," said Presley, matter-of-factly. "We don't bust his balls for it though, because he's saved our asses so many times."

"Yeah, like the time you funnelled half of that 26er of vodka," chuckled Jared. "Someone had to call the ambulance on your ass!"

"I was sick for three days after that," muttered Presley, looking down at the ground. "Fuckin' alcohol poisoning."

Frank looked to each of them. "That's cool," he said. "At least we got a D.D. in case this party sucks and we wanna split."

Chris laughed. "Where the fuck are we gonna go? This is the only thing going on for miles."

Stanley's heart raced a little as he waited to chime in. "Sure, I can D.D.," he said. "Or I can be the last man standing in the middle of all these fine ladies when you suckers are passed out!"

They all erupted in laughter. Stanley was always nervous in situations like this, but he knew how to break the ice and earn the alliance of his fellow young men. Also, not getting drunk and emotional made it less likely for him to end up in a fight situation. He was the sober, reasonable pacifist in a simmering pot of impairment that would gradually boil to chaos over and over again.

And the heat was on. The voices and the music got louder. The stereo shuffled back and forth from hard rock to rap. From Guns N' Roses to Marky Mark and the Funky Bunch to a newly-released Metallica song to C + C Music Factory to Motley Crue to Public Enemy, the soundtrack was a mix of edgy outsider anthems to fluffy pop hits. The former were songs they could relate to and find strength in, while the latter were brief escapes from their often unfavourable realities. Few thought that deeply about the songs, though, and the beats and melodies eventually just became background noise.

Random laughter flared up from various corners of the yard. Discussions escalated and became increasingly laced with profanity. The fire grew higher as more scrap wood was piled on top of the flames. Bottles clanked together in friendly moments of "cheers" and were tossed back into empty cardboard boxes. Girls hugged and brought each other down accidentally with their alcohol-soaked weight and lay on the ground, laughing. Boys stared vacantly into each others eyes with an arm around each other, proclaiming their friendship/brotherhood and vowing to maintain it for life, all the while staying wary of the other and keeping a clenched fist with the other hand just in case.

In just two hours, everyone in Tina King's backyard was very drunk, except Stanley. A handful passed out on the couches and mattresses inside, but their void was filled by other partiers from the rez, many much younger than the rest of the teens there. The thirteen and fourteen-year-olds always waited until the older kids were wasted to show up. Otherwise they wouldn't let them stay. This way, it was easier for the adolescent rez kids to steal beer and bum smokes. The sad truth was this made them much more vulnerable to other horrors at the hands of other youth and even older predators who often also crashed the party later on.

Stanley usually tried to keep an eye out for the young ones. He would tell them to go home, but few ever listened. It only worked on the ones whose parents actually cared that they were out at parties like this. A threat to tattle on them worked wonders. Most of the time, though, he was occupied with drunken and often senseless conversations.

"Stan, man, you're fuckin' awesome!" Tina slurred as she moved in closer to hug him. Her parents were down near Parry Sound for the weekend visiting relatives, so throwing a party was a given. Her brown eyes were watery and bloodshot and her hair was a mess. There was grass all over her Chicago Bulls t-shirt from falling and rolling on the ground.

"Seriously man. You got your shit together. Not like these fuckheads!" she turned to backhand Danny in the belly. He was standing to Stanley's right, talking to Ashley. "Fuck off Tina!" he scowled. She gave him the middle finger and turned back to Stanley.

"*Miigwech* Tina," he said. "I don't think I'm anything special. Anyone here can go to school."

"Yeah but I still got a lot of high school to do," she fretted. "I dropped out last year!"

"Doesn't matter. You got time. You're only 18. No one says you gotta do it at a certain time."

"Yeah maybe. I dunno if I wanna leave here though. I don't know no one nowhere else!"

"That's the only thing I'm worried about. But there's more Indians in cities now. I'm pretty sure I'll be able to meet people down there."

"Where you going again? Barrie?"

"No, Ottawa."

"Aren't you scared?"

"No, not really … maybe a little nervous."

"But even after what happened to Eva?"

He felt his stomach rise and his mouth go dry. He glanced down quickly at his feet before responding. Because she was drunk, he knew he had to choose his words wisely. He took a breath.

"I don't like to think of it that way," he calmly replied. "She was my hero. I miss her every day. I see it as carrying on her work and her memory."

Tina's eyes watered even more. "Aw man that's so sweet. You guys were always a real tight family. Come here, gimme another hug!" She closed in again.

"Just stay away from fuckin' Toronto!"

"Okay Tina. *Miigwech*."

"Hey there's your other sister."

It was like a one-two punch of statements that made his hair stand on end. Tina motioned with her chin over his right shoulder, towards the side of the house where a trio of girls stumbled mildly towards the party core. In the middle was his little sister Maria, just a year younger than him at eighteen. "Fuck sakes," he muttered under his breath.

She hadn't noticed him yet, but he braced for an awkward and potentially volatile conversation. They didn't have much of a positive relationship since Eva died. She rarely stayed at home, and often crashed at their cousin Jamie's place. Jamie was twenty-one and had her own apartment in the community housing building. Maria was legally an adult so she could do what she pleased, and she did. She dropped out of grade eleven late in the fall, and as far as Stanley knew, she had no real plans or ambitions. When she wasn't at home with him and Edgar's family he usually only saw her at parties, so he had no idea what she was up to.

As she approached, Maria saw her brother so she straightened up slightly. Her long, straight black hair draped over a green sweatshirt and a backpack full of beer. Her slanted, moist eyes seemed to rest on high, slender cheekbones. She grew much taller in the last year, and developed a much more adult pretense.

Stanley was still getting used to seeing her growing gradually into a woman. She was the baby of the family. In his eyes, she still acted too childish.

Maria was flanked by two other familiar eighteen-year-olds, her cousin Christina (Presley's sister) and her childhood friend Amanda Smith. They were inseparable as children, and like most bonds borne out of the reserve experience, they maintained it into young adulthood. Maria led the way after she noticed her brother standing beside the party's hostess by the fire. Light-headed and heavy-footed thanks to the beer and the joint they just smoked, she started to focus on adjusting her stride. She figured she better go over and say hi.

"Heeeeey bro," she announced as coolly and smoothly as possible. She didn't see a beer in his hand, so she assumed he was sober. Not wanting to make it any more awkward and uncomfortable that it already was, she aimed to keep the conversation short and sweet.

Stanley smirked and gave a friendly chuckle. "How are you, sis?" he replied. "Feeling no pain tonight?"

"Ah come on. I never feel pain. Just out to have a good time." She took a swig from her beer.

"Well stay outta trouble."

"I always do," she turned to Tina and winked.

Stanley ignored whatever that was supposed to mean. "When you coming home next? I'm taking off in a couple weeks. It would be cool to hang out with you and Ed before I go."

"Yeah I'll be around. Is Alana cooking? Her scone sucks!" She cackled.

Again, Stanley tried to ignore the half-cut commentary. "You should stop by sometime this weekend anyways. Those guys have barely seen you all summer and they miss you."

"Yeah, I'll come over at some point. Dunno when," the truth was Maria felt guilty being hungover or in between benders at her childhood home. Edgar didn't drink anymore, and Stanley was the only teenage guy in their community with a somewhat sober reputation. What was harder, though, was how the depression that came with a hangover tethered itself to the sad memories that seemed to proliferate whenever she returned home, like thick, deep black roots continually feeding a deathly grey orchid. It was a mentally sickening combination that Maria just couldn't bear the older she got.

"Alright, I'll let Ed know," Stanley said.

"Okay. If I come I don't want any fuckin' lectures though!"

"Come on Maria. Don't start."

"Just because you're going to school doesn't mean you're better than me." The alcohol was starting to win against the pot in the emotional battle for her brain.

"I never said that. Calm down."

"Well I know you think it. You show up at these parties and stick up your nose to the rest of us here. Now you're leaving to be a city Indian for good!"

"That's not why I'm leaving. I'm coming back."

An ugly scowl swept across her face. The usual beauty was temporarily gone, due primarily to the depravity that was unleashed from within those destructive bottles.

"How could you do this to your sister?"

"What do you mean? What am I doing to you?"

"Not me! Eva! How could you just forget her? She fuckin' died for us!"

The allegation shocked Stanley. He was speechless. An indisputable rage started creeping in. She's just drunk, he thought to himself.

"Now you're gonna run away from all of us. You're gonna forget about her and the rest of us here. You're a fuckin' asshole Stanley!"

Tina stepped in to interrupt in a vain attempt to relieve the tension. "Maria, that's enough!" she shouted. She stood halfway in front of Stanley.

"Get the fuck outta here bitch, this is none of your business!"

"It's my party, and I don't want people starting shit here. Especially if they're family with each other!"

Maria stepped in closer. "What you gonna do about it then slut?"

"Kicking you the fuck out of here. Leave before I drag you

out by that greasy head of yours!"

Without warning Maria swung her beer bottle at Tina's head. It struck her square in the nose, which started dripping blood in just seconds. It wasn't hard enough to shatter the brown glass, but it dizzied Tina, and the force would certainly leave her with two black eyes. Tina staggered backwards holding her nose. "What the fuck..." she muttered. She held her bloody hands out in front of her face to get an idea of the extent of the damage. Rage swept over her and she pounced on Maria, throwing her to the ground.

They both screamed profanities, and Tina started pounding her fist into Maria's face. Handfuls of hair came out of each other's heads. They rolled on the grass, jostling for position, and threw errant punches in hopes of connecting with the soft brown skin of the other's face. Stanley calmly walked away before he saw anyone come in to break it up.

He made his way towards the deck. Presley stashed one of the cases underneath when the party passed the point of no return. He ducked under the wooden platform and felt around in the dark for the box of beer. He found it up against the foundation, open and half empty. He sat down beside it with his back resting against the cold cinder blocks cemented together to make the wall of the basement. He looked out to the mayhem that was winding down by the fire, but he didn't really see it.

Stanley reached to his right and put his hand in the cardboard box. He pulled out a warm bottle of beer, and without thinking twice twisted off the cap. He brought it slowly up to his lips, smelling the distinct gases escaping and the faint aroma of being able to forget. He opened his mouth and tipped it back. The carbonated, yeasty liquid stung his tongue and warmed his throat all the way down to his stomach. He rested the bottle on his hip and let another mouthful of the warm beer settle and swish about his mouth. He didn't like the taste. He lifted the bottle again to take another drink. His throat hurt as he continued to swallow until it was empty. Another beer followed, and another, and he kept drinking until he blacked out.

The night it was all over, Stanley was sitting at the kitchen table at home, trying to finish an algebra assignment. He couldn't concentrate on it at all, knowing Edgar would soon be home from Toronto. He looked down at the crumpled sheet riddled with sines and cosines, but they failed to clear that emotionally tense cloud at the front of his brain. From behind it they just looked like strange shapes and lines on a white textbook page. He likely didn't need math classes with plans on going into the Humanities at university after high school, but he usually enjoyed the challenge of math problems. To him it was like solving puzzles. There was always an answer.

But the anticipation was just too much to bear. Edgar and their aunt Kathy were on their way back. They were in Toronto for Mark Miller's sentencing hearing that morning. They made the six hour drive the night before to make sure they were there to see Miller off before he went to prison for killing their sister and niece. The whole family had a rough idea of what he would get, but only Edgar and Kathy would find out the actual sentence and then share it with everyone. Otherwise, no one in the family talked much about what happened since her funeral just six months earlier.

Stanley learned most of what he knew about Eva's death from the newspapers. It was a fairly prominent story at the time—promising young Ojibway woman from northern Ontario beaten to death by an affluent young white man in the ominous back alleys of Toronto. Just a day after they found out she was killed, reporters from Toronto and Sudbury started calling the house. Edgar forbade anyone from picking up the phone for a week. He was also reluctant to talk about what happened after picking up Stanley from school that day. All Stanley knew was during that first confusing week was that his sister was beaten up and froze to death, and that a white guy was arrested for doing it.

He gradually put the pieces together when he started reading the papers. Because Miller was a regular at the bar where he met Eva, and because witnesses saw them leaving together, Toronto police were able to find and question Miller just two days after she was found dead. The small bits of evidence slowly piled up against him. He had an untreated broken hand due to the force with which he punched her in the head. Because he was drunk at the time and didn't know she died, he didn't bother to dispose of the sneakers he wore that night. Police found traces of Eva's blood on the right one from his last kick, and they matched the footprints left in the snow. It appeared to be a fairly open and shut case.

But controversy arose. The Crown wanted second degree murder. Miller's high profile lawyer argued for manslaughter. With mounting evidence, his lawyer convinced him to plead guilty to the lesser charge. A deal was struck, and only the sentencing was left. The Crown and the family rallied for the maximum life sentence. Miller's lawyer would argue for just three years on account of his behaviour, social standing, lack of criminal record, the "accidental" nature of the crime, and the flawed fact that there was no minimum sentence for manslaughter in Canada. Edgar and Kathy had driven down to the courthouse on University Avenue for each of Miller's appearances, from his bail hearing to his plea entry to his sentencing hearing, and finally the actual sentencing. The entire family knew this last legal chapter in the tragedy wouldn't bring closure, but Edgar and Kathy had to be there for it.

Stanley only knew Miller from his picture in the paper, which was reprinted that morning under the headline: "Man Guilty of Killing Area Woman to be Sentenced in Toronto". It was a head-and-shoulders shot of him leaving the Toronto courthouse, only a dozen or so blocks from where the crime happened the previous winter. His hair was short and curly. He wore a dark suit and tie. His brow was furrowed and his lips were pulled tightly together. To Stanley, it projected annoyance and anger more than sorrow and remorse. Because the case never went to trial, he didn't really get to learn anything about Miller. No sordid, intimate details of his past life came out in the media— only glowing accolades from his lawyer and his family members who were all too willing to paint him as a stellar member of society. Stanley grew to hate his image.

The screen door on the outside creaked as it was pulled, giving warning that the front door was about to open. Edgar walked in first. His face looked blank. The heaviness in his eyes that had lingered for six months was still there. But he walked in as poised as ever. He kicked off his boots and hung up his coat. Their aunt Kathy—their father's younger sister—stepped out from behind him and did the same. Her eyes were puffy and red under her wide glasses. They both slowly approached the table, and the sharp notes of wood rubbing against tile pierced the still early autumn ambience of the kitchen as they pulled out their chairs. Edgar sat to Stanley's left and Kathy sat across from him. He looked her right in the eyes.

"Five years," is all she said.

Stanley didn't know how to react. His chest sank again, as it did when he first heard about his sister's death, and with the news of each major development since. He waited for his eyes to water, but they didn't. He looked down again at the newspaper, folded open to the page with Miller's picture. He then glanced at his brother.

"We'll find him," Edgar said. "I promise."

Two weeks after the party at Tina's, Stanley was loading his luggage into Edgar's brown station wagon. They were packing it up to make the drive to Ottawa. Edgar and Alana hosted a going away supper for him the night before. They had Indian Tacos—rez-specific food that he likely wouldn't have again until he was back at Thanksgiving. It was the first time all four remaining Gibson siblings had eaten together for months, and it would be the last time for a while. Norman even showed up from Sudbury. Stanley thought he had been in the Soo. His older brother was unreliable and unpredictable, but he didn't care as long as they were all there for his departure. Maria didn't mention anything about their confrontation at Tina's. He chose to deliberately forget about that night altogether, still ashamed that he got drunk and passed out under the deck.

Edgar, his wife and son walked down the front steps of the house. "Ready to go?" the older brother asked. "Yep, looks like it," Stanley replied matter-of-factly. "Alright then."

"You better not go without kissing your nephew bye!" commanded Alana with a smile. Stanley walked up to meet them as they reached the bottom of the stairs. "See ya later buddy!" he smiled, as he grabbed the toddler's tiny hand and shook it. He kissed the top of his forehead and opened his arms to hug Alana. "You'll be great," she said, struggling to choke back tears as she squeezed him tightly. "We're really proud of you. Don't forget, you can call anytime." Seeing her emotional drove a hard lump into Stanley's throat. She forced a wide smile across her light brown cheeks, brushing her curly bangs from her eyes. In the past two years she had become a de facto older sister to him.

"I'll be back in just over a month. It won't be long," Stanley promised, as he walked around to the passenger side of the car.

"Be careful around those white women!" she yelled. He raised his arms with his palms up, as if to give an air of naive innocence before smirking and climbing into the car. Edgar kissed his wife and son and got in the driver's side. He started the engine and they pulled out of the driveway.

Stanley turned around to look as the house faded into the green leaves and brush, unsure of when he'd actually be back.

MARIA
Spring 1993

Maria sat on the front steps of the Gibson house, elbows resting on her knees as she smoked a cigarette. Her bare tanned forearms rubbed against the coarse cotton material of her long black skirt. She didn't usually wear dresses or skirts, but Kathy told her on the phone the night before to make sure she had one on for the morning. Maria wore a pair of jean shorts underneath both for comfort and to easily get out of the skirt whenever and wherever she was finally allowed to. She wore a navy blue button-up short sleeve shirt overtop. Her long, dark hair was back in a tight ponytail, and sunglasses rested on the top of her head, partially concealing the sharp part in the middle of her scalp.

It was a mild late-May morning and the sun was still concealed by the thick vegetation to her right. Reddish-orange rays poked through, occasionally flashing into her squinting dark brown eyes. Various songbirds chirped from the trees above, weaving a beautiful random medley together that embodied the refreshing sense of renewal that seemed to descend like a comforting dew around her.

Maria took a long drag of the cigarette, and chuckled to herself as she exhaled. It was seven o'clock on a Saturday morning. Her routine over the past few years would have had her either passed out, heading home, or still partying at this hour on the weekend. She was coming up on three months off of booze, and she was feeling pretty good—actually better than she had felt in a really long time. Her aunt Kathy asked her to go for a medicine walk this weekend, and she was excited about it. She wasn't as thrilled about the early departure, but she knew it was part of learning about the old ways.

She tried to peer through the trees to the main road to see if Kathy was approaching. Without the birds, it would be eerily silent on a morning like this. There was no wind to rustle the leaves or to push waves into the shore. Although the lake was about half a kilometre south of the house, the rhythm of the waves washing over the yellow sand was always a dominant sound in this corner of the community. It was like its natural heartbeat; a reminder that life still thrived here.

Maria was slowly once again learning to be hopeful. She kicked booze because of an ugly incident at a memorial feast for Eva in March. Edgar decided that they should get together once a year around the time of Eva's death to honour her memory and send her positive thoughts and prayers in the Spirit World. It had been four years since she was killed, and he felt the rest of the family needed to get on a path to healing.

Stanley couldn't make it because of school but Norman said he'd be there. Maria didn't really understand what Edgar was trying to do, and since she only planned on making a brief appearance, she started drinking early in the day. It was also on a Saturday, after all. When she showed up, Edgar sent her away because she smelled like booze. She protested, tempers flared quickly, and out of the blue she took a swing at Alana, who was trying to escort her inside to put her to bed. She didn't connect, but the whole scene was enough to make her deeply remorseful the next day. She apologized to her brother and his wife and agreed to take a break from drinking. Nearly three months on, it was going well.

A faint crackling of rubber rolling on gravel slowly got louder from out on the main road. She hadn't heard a car since she went outside to sit and wait on the steps, so Maria thought it was most likely Kathy. The wheels slowed as they approached the end of the road leading to the house. Her grey minivan turned the corner and rolled up to the driveway and turned in. Her large trademark prescription sunglasses covered nearly half of her face. Just the previous fall, she traded in her old green station wagon for her new minivan, and it was her pride and joy. It had power windows and cruise control. A braid of sweetgrass hung from the rearview mirror.

Kathy pressed down on the tiny lever by the door handle to open the window. She stuck her head out. "*Kwe! Aambe maajaadaa!*" she shouted. "Let's go!" She giggled and her whole upper body heaved as it usually did. She stuck her head back in the van. Maria picked up the blue cloth bag and the grey hooded sweater at her feet and bounded down the stairs and up to the van to get in the passenger's side.

"*Aaniish na?*" Kathy asked. "How's it going?

"Oh pretty good," said Maria. "I was just laughing to myself before you showed up. I'm not used to getting up this early."

"You're probably usually just getting home at this time!"

"Yeah, I used to anyways," the niece laughed awkwardly and looked out the window. The aunt shifted the car into reverse and backed out of the driveway. She pulled out on to the main road and turned north.

Spring had just reached full bloom, and the sides of the road were thick with greenery that hung over the ditches. It almost seemed like nature's protective buffer from the loud, obscene and often dangerous activity that drove up and down the road. At the same time, the thick leaves provided a false sense of security for careless drivers. But crashing into these great wooden pillars was often fatal. The Birchbark rez grieved many drunk driving deaths over the past few decades, and most of them happened on the main road.

The sun began to peak above the line of trees. "So where are we going anyways?" asked Maria. Kathy adjusted her shades and checked the integrity of her tall hairdo, sprayed tight and stiff just half an hour earlier. "Well, I was thinking of taking you into the bush on the north side of the highway just up past the trading post. That's where my auntie Jean took us as kids to show us the medicines."

"Alright, cool."

"Then maybe we'll go for lunch at Henry's. My treat."

"Whoa big spender! Did you win the lottery or something?"

"Not yet. Consider it part of your birthday present." Maria's birthday was coming up in June.

"Well chi-miigwech! I haven't eaten there in years."

It was an annual tradition for Bill and Clara to take their kids for supper at Henry's on Maria's birthday. She was the youngest—the baby—and therefore slightly spoiled compared to the rest of the children. But the others looked forward to it regardless, because it was always a big meal and they were all allowed to get whatever they wanted. The boys usually went for the buffet. Seeing who could eat the most was always an ongoing competition among them. Norman usually won, but by the time Stanley was fourteen, he was crowned the new champion. By then he was taller than his older brothers, and his adolescence had given him the greater appetite. The tradition died later that year with Bill and Clara's fatal accident.

"So how's work going?" Maria attempted to make small talk.

"Oh okay. You know how it is working in a place this small. Always lots of fires to put out." Kathy was the assistant to the band manager, the right hand to the most loved/hated person on the rez besides the Chief.

"You taking any time off this summer?"

"We'll see. Depends what Harvey wants to do and when he can get off from the mill." Her husband worked at the pulp mill outside of Espanola. "What about you? What are your plans?"

"I'm gonna see what kinda jobs the band opens up for the summer. I don't wanna have to go into town for work. That would suck. I wouldn't mind getting on with maintenance. It'd be a good chance to spend a lotta time outside."

"What about school? Gonna go back in the fall?"

"I was thinking about it …"

Maria didn't attend high school at all during the current school year. Being twenty years old, she felt a sense of shame and futility around the thought of even walking through the halls again. She had dropped out at different points in each of the two previous years, so she still had a full year to go in order to get enough credits for her grade twelve diploma. It seemed like an insurmountable challenge just a year earlier. But now that her head was clearer, it seemed more feasible. Plus, she was getting bored with her newly-clean lifestyle.

"Well that's good," said Kathy. "You're a very smart young woman. You have a good heart. You have a lot of great gifts you can share with people." She stopped herself there. The last thing she wanted to do this morning was lecture her niece. This was a special time for reconnecting, and she wanted to savour the moments and impart some of the great teachings she carried proudly. She and Harvey were never able to have kids, so she held her nieces and nephews very dearly, especially her brother Bill's children.

The sharp rumbling under the tires became a soft hum as the gravel road became asphalt. That meant within moments, they'd be at the turnoff to Highway 17. Kathy pulled the signal lever down to go left, but patiently waited for the transport truck barreling towards them before stepping on the gas. The truck rumbled through and she stomped on the pedal, making sure they were safely in traffic before any other massive, powerful machines surprised them. Turning onto the highway in a vehicle always made Maria nervous. It's the last thing her parents did before they died. In seconds, they were up to speed, and Kathy proudly pressed the "on" button in the cruise controls on the steering wheel.

Highway 17 along the north shore of Lake Superior is renowned for its beauty. Not far west from the town of Massey, it hugs the shoreline. When the water isn't visible, the drive is defined by beautiful rocky, evergreen landscapes. It's a spectacle nearly year-round, but it's truly a sight to behold from the late spring, when the flora is vibrant, to the early fall, when the leaves change colours. It goes from a lively, lush, shimmering landscape of wildlife, vegetation, and sparkling water to a fiery natural seasonal segue. As such, the towns and reserves along the route are havens for tourists, especially in the summer.

The grey minivan rolled along the smooth asphalt at ninety kilometres an hour, past tall roadside signs advertising motels, resorts, campgrounds, and restaurants. The road curved gradually around rock cuts, dipped and peaked as it carved through the demanding terrain of the Canadian Shield. There were lookout spots at high points on the south side of the highway. Fruit and other produce stands were just beginning to set up shop at major intersections. Hitchhikers stood firmly with thumbs out and backpacks at their feet, trying their luck in either direction, holding cardboard signs that said "SSM", "Wawa", and "T-Bay" in one direction, and "Sudbury", "Barrie", and "T.O." in the other.

After about fifteen minutes Kathy signalled right to turn

north onto Chimong Road. "Goin' up the big loon!" she said. Maria smiled and nodded, not really understanding. As usual, the paved road turned to gravel less than fifty metres in, and the familiar crunches and knocks of rocks in the wheel well picked back up. Kathy drove over a slight hill, and then safely pulled over on to the shoulder.

As soon as they got out of the van and stepped onto the road, the comforting scent of sweetgrass almost overwhelmed them. It grew wildly on the outer edges of the ditch, closer to the brush leading up to a slight hill into the forest. It wasn't the prettiest spot for the medicine to grow, but it tended to flourish there because of the water and near constant sun. Even the slightest breeze caused its long green blades to sway peacefully in unison. Maria was very familiar with the scent; she just hadn't savoured it in a long time. It flowed like long green hair in the wind, and it mesmerized her.

"That's *wiingashk*," she said. "Sweetgrass. You know it. We'll pick some on our way back before we leave. There are some other things I want to show you in there first." She motioned with her head to the ridge in the bush. Maria threw her blue drawstring bag over her shoulder and led the way. She hopped over the pool of water in the ditch onto the other side. Then turned to her shorter and rounder aunt, and held out her hand to help her over.

"*Shkinaa*!" Kathy protested. "I'm not that old!" Maria giggled and turned back to the bush and walked up the slight hill. The trees filtered a light late-spring breeze the deeper they got into the forest, and it soon became pleasantly calm. The temperature was rising already and Maria was still comfortable in short sleeves. She smiled to herself as she navigated through the old trees and low brush. She made sure the long skirt didn't tangle in any of the thorn bushes or didn't catch any burrs. Kathy walked silently behind her, enjoying the tranquility and sanctity of their traditional refuge.

They walked for a few more minutes, soaking in the beauty of the season of rebirth. Chickadees and blue jays fluttered from tree to tree. The sharp, rapid-fire knocks of the woodpecker's dig for food high above was like an accelerated metronome. Any other ground wildlife would have heard them rumbling through the bush from hundreds of metres away, so there was no trace of deer or bears. Kathy and Maria were the solitary mammals for the time being.

Kathy walked ahead to a small clearing between four large birch trees, almost symmetrically placed around three large, flat rocks. "Let's sit here for a bit," she said, pointing ahead. She approached the one farthest from them, took off her sunglasses, and sat down. Maria took the rock right across from her.

"Let's smudge. Give me the medicine."

Maria took the blue cloth bag from her shoulder and handed it to Kathy. Kathy untied the bow that closed the top of the bag and pulled it open with her fingers. She reached in and pulled out an abalone shell and set it down on the rock beside her. The iridescence of the inside surface was accentuated by the elevating sun. It sparkled with pink, purple, and blue specks, and had Maria's eyes transfixed. Kathy reached back into the bag and pulled out a neatly rolled red cloth handkerchief nearly as long as her forearm. She set it down gently beside the shell, and reached back in for a small box of matches. She put her hand in again and grabbed a long, rectangular fold of birchbark that she placed on the other side of the shell. Finally, she pulled out a small leather pouch with beaded red and green flowers on the front. They all lay neatly in a row to her left.

"Here, take some *semaa*," she said as she handed Maria the leather pouch. Maria untied the leather string and pulled out a large pinch of tobacco. She nestled it firmly in her right hand and squeezed. "Put it in your left hand," Kathy said. "Your left hand is closer to your heart."

"Oh yeah, right." Maria replied, slightly embarrassed that she forgot this ceremonial step. She opened her left hand and carefully let the brown grains drop into her palm. She wiped her right palm on the outside of her left baby finger, and used her right forefinger to assemble the tobacco into one tight, solid offering in her left palm. She rolled her left fingers over it and sat looking at her closed fist for a moment.

Kathy unrolled the red cloth on her lap to reveal long stalks of dried, grey sage. Maria could smell it from two metres away. It was strong. Kathy picked four stocks from the bunch and broke them in half with both hands. She gathered the halved stocks together and broke them again in the middle. Placing the handful of sage gently in the shell beside her, she reached across the shell and opened the birchbark fold to reveal a neatly positioned eagle feather with four thin ribbons tied to the bottom: one yellow, one red, one black, and one white. She opened the box of matches and struck one. The sharp pop of the ignition and the immediate odour of sulphur that penetrated her nostrils was almost obscene in the midst of this serenity, but it was necessary.

She let the flame crawl slightly up the tiny stick, and picked up the shell with her left hand, then slowly guided the match under the small pile of sage and waited for it to catch. In less than a second a bright orange flame jumped up from the dried plant. She shook out the match and let the sage burn for a few seconds. Placing the bowl in her right hand, she reached with her left to grab the stem of the feather.

"This is *mashkodewashk*," she declared. "Sage. Have you smudged with this before?"

"No, I don't think so," said Maria.

"You've probably used sweetgrass before. This is stronger. It has more power to cleanse your spirit. It can remove some of the negativity that you've been carrying with you."

Maria remembered smelling it from the corner of her room, after Kathy gave her the medicine bundle the week earlier. Kathy wanted her spirit to become familiar with the medicines before teaching her about them. It smelled a little like marijuana to her, but she wouldn't dare mention that to her aunt.

Kathy let the flames subside and fanned them out with the feather. She fanned the smoking leaves and stalks a few more times as the thick, potent grey smoke gradually billowed from the shell. The strong, smoothing scent soon made its way across to Maria and she was intrigued.

"As an *Anishinaabekwe*, you have a special connection to

these medicines, my girl, and you have a gift deep down inside you to find them and to use them to nurture the ones around you. As your auntie, it's my job to help you find that gift."

She walked over to Maria. "Stand up," she gently commanded. Maria took her own sunglasses off the top of her head, set them down beside her on the rock, and stood up dutifully with as much stoicism as she could muster. She held her left hand to her side just above her hip with the tobacco resting in her palm. Kathy fanned the burning sage a few more times and eased the shell closer to Maria. She held it still, close to Maria's chest.

With her right hand, Maria waved the smoke of the sage towards her. She directed it to her face, her shoulders, her chest, her torso, and her legs. She ran her hand through her hair as if to wash it. This was a timeless purification ceremony, and although Maria could count on one hand—maybe two—how many times she had done it in her life, she oddly felt as if these motions and this ritual were ingrained in her spirit. She was still unsure whether she believed in all that stuff, but this seemed so natural to her.

"Turn around," said Kathy. Maria did, and her aunt fanned more of the cleansing smudge up and down her back. She touched the feather on either shoulder, and Maria responded with "*miigwech*." Maria turned back around and Kathy handed her the shell and the feather. She conducted the same process for her aunt. Kathy thanked her as well, and took back the shell. She set it back in its place on the rock and sat down. Maria took her seat across from her.

"It's quiet back here," remarked Maria, breaking the silence.

"Mmmmhmmmm," acknowledged Kathy.

"You come back here much?"

"Oh every once in a while. A few times a spring and more often in the summer anyways. Even if I don't need anything I come back here just for the peace and quiet. It's nice."

"It is."

Not that the slight bustle of the rez was overtly loud, but they both seemed to agree the tranquility was nicer in wide open spaces, rather than when confined by the mouldy drywall or cheap particle board that made the walls in their homes. "Your great auntie Jeanie used to take me out here when I was a girl. She said this was the best place to collect the medicines. We used to walk all the way up here from Birchbark. We would get up right when the sun was rising because it took so long to get here. And we wanted to make sure we got back before dark. Can't trust drivers on the highway."

"Whoa, how long did it take to walk here? It took us about twenty minutes driving."

"Oh, maybe about two hours. We would leave with empty sacks over our shoulders and pack them pretty full while we were here."

"Wasn't it hard walking back with all those bags?"

"No my girl. The medicines aren't heavy. Their abilities are heavy. But the creator packs a lot of power in these little packages to make it easier for us to carry them around."

"How often did Auntie Jeanie take you up here?"

"Well, it really depended on how she was feeling. She tried to at least once a year though. The first time was when I was twelve, I think."

"What do you mean it depended on how she was feeling?" Maria felt oddly curious and a little guilty about asking so many questions.

"Well your auntie had a tough life. Just like your grandma and grandpa, she had to go to residential school. Her mother, your great grandmother, showed her the medicines when she was even younger. She was just a little girl, maybe only six or seven years old. But then she was taken away to the school in Spanish."

Maria looked down at the ground, ashamed that she pried into a tragic and difficult chapter of her family's past. Kathy noticed her reticence.

"Don't worry my girl, it's something we all have to talk about and deal with. Even though the priests and nuns beat your auntie for speaking her language, she still held that knowledge of the medicines with her. She told me once that she and the other girls used to share that knowledge with each other behind the backs of their abusers. They wanted to make sure it never disappeared. They would even use code words in English to quiz each other about what each medicine does. Pretty smart eh?"

"Yeah, that's really cool."

"By the time she got out though, she was confused and angry just like everyone else. But she wanted to make sure the knowledge she worked hard to keep alive carried on. When she came back to Birchbark everything was a mess. People were drinking all the time. There were fights. No one wanted to speak the language. It was an ugly time.

"But when we all came along—me and your other aunties— she had someone to share it with. She waited until we were *shkiniikwewag* though—young women. Your grandpa didn't stand for it. 'Those old ways are dead' he'd say. 'Don't teach those kids that witchcraft.' But he didn't stand in her way. He would turn a blind eye whenever she came to get us with those big sacks. I think deep down he wanted the old ways to live on too."

Maria took a deep breath. "I always forgot how hard it must have been back then."

"It's still hard now," reassured Kathy. "Those residential schools are the reason we still have problems today. When you're told everything about who you are is wrong, it's gonna do some damage. For a long time. That's why you can't speak the language well today. That's why you've never smudged with sage until now. It takes a long time to wash that shame and abuse away."

Maria knew all of this. She just never chose to really acknowledge or accept it. It was easier to try to forget, especially with the losses her family endured over the past seven years—starting with the deaths of her parents, Bill and Clara. The night they died and the months thereafter were a foggy haze for Maria. She didn't remember much of what happened. Instead, she subconsciously blocked that trauma from her memory. The years that followed were defined by chaos and confusion. In some ways it brought her and her siblings closer together, but it also drove them apart. And they had never been so distant as they were then—seven years after losing their loving caregivers, mentors, and guides, and four years after losing their beloved sister Eva. Her eyes darted about the trees surrounding them before finally settling on the intent, concerned gaze deep within her aunt's hazel eyes.

"You're carrying a lot of pain with you, my girl," she said. "You need to let it out of you. You've already lived through so much at such a young age. I'm here for you. I want you to talk about it."

Maria felt her invisible emotional walls shoot up quickly. She never talked about her losses or her anger and sadness. She just didn't want to. It was easy to force them into the corner of her mind and bury them with even more mental dirt as the years went on. She shifted her seat on the rock and cleared her throat. Her aunt cut in before she could begin.

"Let's offer our tobacco before we go on," Kathy said. "Come over to this birch tree." They stood up at the same time and Kathy led Maria to the birch tree to the east of their small spiritual shelter. Kathy looked at the white bark randomly scarred with horizontal grey lines. She followed the pattern up to the branches lush with bunches of spade-like leaves. "This is the *wiigwaasitig*," she said. "The birch tree. You probably noticed a lot around growing up. It's very important to our culture and our stories. Here, look." With her thumbnail, she scratched a few small markings into the soft white bark. "See how easy it is to draw on them?"

"Yeah, I used to mark them up with my initials when I was a kid," said Maria. "I always thought that was so cool."

"Well, traditionally our people used the birchbark to record stories and other important information. You may have heard that we Anishinaabe had an 'oral tradition' of passing down our stories in culture with the spoken word, and that we didn't write anything. That's not totally true. We used to draw on this *wiigwaas* to have records of those stories. We kept them in scrolls. They could be anything—maps, hunting guides, important stories about creation, or clan stories."

"That's really cool."

"Traditionally, in our route along the north shore, we always stopped where our rez is now to get birchbark for the scrolls. We called that area *Wiigwaasitiging*—or the place of the birch trees. That's why the rez is known simply as 'Birchbark' today."

Maria looked all the way up the tree. This knowledge was a little mind-blowing. Kathy spoke again. "Let's put down our *semaa* to give thanks for our community and the medicines we are going to take today. Just say '*gchi-manidoo miigwech*' as you put it down."

Kathy leaned over and opened her left hand to let the tobacco fall to the base of the tree. She wiped the remnants from her palm with her other hand. "*Gchi-manidoo miigwech,*" said Maria, as she leaned over to do the same. Kathy turned to take her place on the rock again, and Maria followed. They sat across from each other once again.

"I'm here today to teach you," said the aunt. She carried on bluntly. "I'm not here to lecture you. I know that's what Ed does. But he doesn't know how to help right now. He cares so much about you. I think if he could take all that bad stuff away by snapping his fingers, he would. I'm here to show you those important things my auntie showed me. It's an honour for me to share them with you. But I need to make sure you're in a good way before I give you the gift of the medicines."

Maria felt tears in her eyes. Kathy was sitting intensely still with her hands folded on her lap.

"You've been struggling, I know. You haven't been living in a good way. It's not your fault. But when you saw things going downhill, you made a choice to get better. I'm proud of you. I know you've been staying away from the bottle for a while. And I can see a change in you. You look like a twenty-year-old woman again. Before you had bitterness in your eyes. It made you look old and angry. You looked tired. I even looked younger than you!"

Maria chuckled quietly at Kathy's attempt at comic relief. It eased some of the tense sadness washing over her like a storm's wave on Lake Huron. Kathy continued.

"In our old Anishinaabe ways we talked about these things

all the time. That's how we healed. We shared our struggles in sacred places like the sweatlodge. But all those traditions were taken away from us. What were we supposed to do then? Drink the pain away? It's a quick fix but it works only temporarily. That's why your brother Norman is still struggling. He's keeping reality away for as long as he can. But I want you to remember you didn't cause these problems. You just need to know that you control how you handle them. Before you do that, you have to talk. So now it's your turn."

Kathy leaned to her side, posting her right arm on the rock. She turned her eyes down affectionately to her niece in an attempt to help her feel comfortable, but not vulnerable. The remaining sage smouldered in the shell, letting the powerful medicine linger in the still early morning spring air. The sun rose ever higher into the leafy canopy of the trees, softening its dazzle on their naturally squinting eyes.

After the momentary lapse of sadness, Maria looked down at the grass and twigs on the ground again and her face hardened. She cleared her throat once more. She looked to her left, not really seeing anything, but physically preparing herself to let loose some of the things that had been bothering her for years. She looked back up at Kathy.

"I guess …" she started. "I guess I'm just really angry. I think that's where it all comes from. And when I'm not angry, I'm pretty fuckin' sad. Sorry for swearing."

Kathy appeared unfazed.

"I don't know if I've ever really been happy since I was a kid. I feel like the most important people in my life were taken from me, and the rest just abandoned me. And then I feel like I'm just feeling sorry for myself, and I get angry again. At myself."

She wiped her eyes with her fingers and rubbed her nose against the back of her bare forearm, exposing the lighter underside to her aunt.

"It's not fair. I miss my mom. I miss my dad. I miss Eva." Her lip quivered and a tear fell from her high cheekbone. Kathy was still amazed how much Maria reminded her of her older sister Eva. She had that same strong, chiseled face that portrayed both stern dignity and soft compassion.

"And I wanna kill that fucker who took her from us!"

Kathy let her keep going but Maria paused. The tears seemed to retreat back into her eyes and the rage reappeared. She mourned for her sister every day. But because of how she died, she felt like she would never get closure. As long as Mark Miller's heart continued to beat, there was no justice.

Maria was home sick that day. She wasn't really sick, she just didn't want to go to school. But she wasn't playing hooky on a Friday to extend her weekend. She was treading in a dark, deep pool of depression that she had been wading into since Bill and Clara's accident. Once Eva left home to go to school, Maria fell right in. It became a debilitating illness, but only a few people discussed or even legitimized it, especially on the rez.

She lay on her bed in the basement room staring at the ceiling. There was a small letterbox of a window in the corner above her feet. There was a black towel pinned into the drywall around it to keep the natural light out. The snow on the ground outside amplified the overcast sky, and penetrated the towel through its worn holes, peeking above and underneath it. The light annoyed Maria, but she didn't have the energy or the desire to find another towel to pin overtop.

The room itself was silent. A New Kids on the Block tape sat in the tape deck of her boombox on the desk on the other side of the room, but it hadn't been played in days. A stack of other cassettes slowly started collecting dust beside it. Maria just didn't feel like listening to Paula Abdul, Bon Jovi, or Roxette that winter. Boredom just made it too hard to ignore the sadness and the three wide gaps in her everyday life.

Edgar had become her guardian and her father figure when she was thirteen and orphaned by a drunk driver on the highway that connected them to the outside world. She loved her brother, and knew he had an incredibly difficult job, having to raise her and Stanley while Norman took off to do who knows what. Thankfully Alana moved in not long after Eva left. It was tough for Maria to accept this new normal in her home—but she appreciated having another woman in the house.

Now, at sixteen, she needed that influence more than ever, with her older sister and hero following her dreams in the big city. In the dark years following the tragedy that took their parents from them, Eva was a beacon of hope. Her hard work was paying off, and it especially inspired Stanley and Maria. She was just a month and a half from returning home for the summer, and Maria was thrilled. Remembering this while sprawled on her bed in a trench of pity brought a faint smile to Maria's face.

The phone rang upstairs. She could hear it through the plywood that separated the basement from the top half of the house. The wooden barrier cut out the high end of the phone's electronic ringtone, making it sound like a muffled buzz of just bass. It rang once more before she heard a few short footsteps pace from the living room to the kitchen to get it. She heard a low voice answer, and although it was tough to hear distinctly, the rhythm and cadence hinted that it was Edgar saying "*aanii!*" It was a house originally big enough for a family their size, but the thin barriers between the rooms sometimes compromised privacy, often in awkward and uncomfortable ways.

Edgar was silent for a moment but kept talking to the person on the other end of the line in short bursts. Maria tuned out these noises after a dozen or so seconds. The buzz of the phone snapped her out of her reminiscent daze only briefly, and now her mind was ready to go back there in hopes of staving off the sadness. She turned to her side and tried to think of something else—anything else. All of her homework was already done and she didn't feel like reading for fun. Suddenly she heard what sounded like inexplicable sobbing coming from upstairs. Within seconds the lighter footsteps of Alana hurriedly creaked from the bathroom to the kitchen. "What's wrong?" she frantically asked Edgar. Those two sounds were easily discernible for Maria.

Edgar mumbled something that she couldn't make out. With a futile attempt to hold back the rush of tears, he tried to continue speaking. Maria's heart started to race and she could feel and hear the pounding in her ears. She gripped the quilt beneath her firmly with both hands at her sides. Something was clearly wrong. Alana began to cry with Edgar at a much higher pitch. The muffled chorus of sorrow from the floor above sickened Maria. What now? I can't handle anymore.

The sorrow seemed to stop abruptly and Maria could hear feet moving quickly towards the basement door. The doorknob turned sharply, piercing the silence of the open lower level of the house, carrying quickly down the stairs and through Maria's own open bedroom door. Oh no, she thought. She was about to get the news. Edgar's heavy feet stepped down onto the wooden stairs first, followed by his partner. There were fifteen steps from upstairs to the basement floor. Maria knew this well. She used the stairs to learn how to count when she was a little girl. Fifteen steps from the dark, cold basement to the bright, warm, and loud main floor. From the moment she learned numbers she counted aloud every time she lumbered up the stairs with her tiny limbs. Fifteen was the highest she could count up to until she went to kindergarten. Now, she was counting down from fifteen, awaiting what would certainly be a terrible true story.

The creaks of the wooden steps dissolved in the damp air of the basement, and once Edgar and Alana reached the concrete floor their feet became inaudible. Maria closed her eyes and took a deep breath. She opened them and turned her head right to face the door. Edgar was wearing a white t-shirt and grey sweatpants, and random strands of hair hung at the sides of his face, having come loose from his tight ponytail. He pouted, and his eyes glistened. Alana's hair was wet and stringy having showered minutes earlier. Her hair left wet spots on the shoulders of her red t-shirt. After looking into Maria's eyes, she started crying again.

Edgar walked to the edge of her bed and sat down. He put his hand on her fist, still clenched to the quilt. He was close enough to look back and forth between her eyes. "The Toronto Police just called," he said. "They had some bad news," his voice broke. He inhaled sharply through his nose while Alana fell to her knees, cupping her face in her hands.

Edgar looked in Alana's direction and swallowed hard before turning back to his baby sister.

"Your sister's dead."

Kathy got up and walked across to Maria's rock. She sat down beside her crying niece and put her arm around her. It had been more than four years since Eva's death, but the memories and the emotions of those times hadn't faded. Kathy cried too. She squeezed Maria's right shoulder hard, and pulled her in close. She caressed her smooth black hair with her other hand, and kissed the top of her head. Maria's hair smelled like the sage smudge.

Her body heaved while the fluids of sorrow streamed from her face. She wiped her eyes and blew her nose periodically with a blue handkerchief that Kathy handed her. This was a physical release. It was a therapeutic purging of buried negativity. Maria had stomped on this mound of repressed grief repeatedly over the years—the last two especially—to ensure that it never emerged. Kathy had sensed that and grew increasingly worried. Too often, Maria had been showing up at family gatherings reeking of alcohol, either drunk or hungover. There were stories of dangerously epic parties almost every week. The gossipers relayed stories about her abusive relationships with other young men in their community who were on parallel paths to destruction. She hoped this trip into the bush would help her niece get better.

"It's okay, my girl," she assured her. "Nobody deserves this much loss in their lifetime. Especially not you."

Maria pressed her head closer into Kathy's shoulder. There was grief and mourning and affection in the months right after Eva's death. But Maria noticed it fade quickly in those around her once the legal saga unfolded. Initially, Edgar selected himself as the family's sole representative in the courtroom. It took him two days to drive back from the first bail hearing in Toronto. He never said why and no one talked about it. Kathy insisted she join him for the remainder of the legal proceedings and he reluctantly agreed. By then Norman was gone and Stanley retreated to books and music. It was like an unspoken moratorium was placed on discussing their sister's violent death. As such, the mourning and subsequent healing was impeded, and Maria hadn't cried soberly over the loss of her sister until this moment in the bush with her aunt.

Maria calmed, but her throat was sore and her nose was raw. Kathy patted her shoulder once more and rubbed it up and down with her palm. The contact of their skin was comforting for both. "A lot of us let you down," Kathy said. "We didn't really know how to deal with all that. Your parents were taken. And then just when we all thought we could move on, your sister was taken too. We should have really been there for each other. But we fell apart. And you're the one who suffered. I'm sorry my girl."

"Don't be sorry," Maria sniffed. "It's nobody's fault."

"You feel okay to go for a walk?"

"Yeah, let's go. I'll feel better."

"Okay then."

Kathy got up stepped back over to the rock she was sitting on and packed the shell, feather, tobacco, sage, and matches back into the blue drawstring bag. Maria stood up and gave her eyes one last rub with the handkerchief. She cleared her throat and tugged at the bottom of her shirt to straighten it. The air was getting much warmer and the comforting sun rose even higher. "Ah, the *giizis* is shining bright on us today," said Kathy, nodding up in the direction of the sun.

"*Maajaadaa*," she said. "Let's go."

Kathy started walking in the direction they were already going before stopping to smudge and Maria followed. She didn't say anything, as she found talking and walking often left her winded. For a woman in her late 40s, she wasn't in the greatest shape. Maria enjoyed the silence for now, after the intense discussion they just had. Maria actually didn't say much, but it was enough to relieve her. She felt lighter on her feet as they stepped on the coarse ground of small stones, broken twigs, and branches. The sun beamed down warmly on her already darkening face, and she smiled.

They approached a short cedar tree—only four metres high—and stopped. "This is the cedar tree, or *giizhikatig*," proclaimed Kathy. "Can you smell it?" Maria inhaled deeply through her nostrils. The sharp evergreen scent tingled through her nasal passages and seemed to clear them. Maria was fairly familiar with the tree and its medicine already (Edgar made her cedar tea once when she was sick), but she wanted to learn more about it.

"This medicine is a special gift from Mother Earth," continued Kathy, as she picked a few thin, hard stems of leaves off the fan-like branches. She cleaned the ends of the brown stems off of the small, dense dark green foliage and handed it to Maria. "We call it *giizhik*. Here, taste it." Maria put it in her mouth and chewed a few times with her left molars. It tasted much like it smelled, and as the juices dripped down the back of her tongue to her throat it seemed to have the same refreshing and relieving effect. "You've had cedar tea before, eh?" Kathy asked her.

"Yeah Ed made it for me once. It was good."

"It's strong medicine. You can also take a bath in it. It helps cleanse and purify your body. We also use it when we offer our tobacco in thanks in the sweatlodge. It eases everything around it. It's a little like the sage. But it's a different medicine and we use it in a different way."

Maria nodded and chewed a few more times. Kathy instructed her to grab a few handfuls to put in one of the small cloth pouches in the bag over her shoulder. She showed her how to clean the twig remnants from the leaves, which was essential prior to making tea.

They continued into the bush, and over the next hour, Kathy pointed out more plants and flowers and their healing properties. The sumac (or *pwaaganatig*, in Ojibway), she told Maria, can also be made into a tea. The clusters of tiny red fruits were easy to pick, as long as the plant wasn't too high. They looked like dark red light bulbs at the end of long, stringy branches. At one particular plant, they were much too high for Kathy to reach, so Maria easily picked two and put them in another small bag.

"Save those for another time," said Kathy. "I'll show you how to make that tea. It's really good for you." Maria enjoyed learning about these natural surroundings. She felt a budding sense of purpose within them.

As they walked, Kathy stopped abruptly and leaned over. Maria was looking through the trees and didn't notice. She bumped into Kathy's behind and nearly knocked her over. Kathy posted her hand on the ground to stop herself from going face-first into the grass. "*Shkinaa!*" she scolded. "Watch where you're going!"

"Sorry!" Maria apologized, with a strong emphasis on the second syllable.

"Holay, just trying to hump me from behind like a horny *nimoosh!*"

They both laughed.

"Anyways, see these dandelions?"

Maria looked down to see the yellow flowers punctuated throughout the shaggy grass in the small clearing.

"Our people even used these as medicine for your skin. If you get bad acne, you can make an ointment with them."

"Really?"

"Yep and it works really good too."

"Why didn't you tell me this when I was fifteen!"

"You didn't ask!"

"As if!"

Maria hip-checked Kathy as she walked up beside her to pick a few. "Shouldn't bend over so far like that next time. You'll give some of the dogs around the rez a real big target!"

"*Shkinaa!*" Kathy scolded as she playfully slapped her butt with the back of her hand. They put a couple of handfuls of dandelions in the bag and started walking back to the van parked on the side of Chimong Road.

When they got there, Kathy unlocked the back gate and opened it. Maria gently placed the much fuller blue medicine bag on the floor. "Leave it open," Kathy instructed. "We'll put some *wiingashk* back here before we leave." She led the way back over to the small ridge they originally climbed up and stopped in front of the long, flowing sweetgrass. The sweet smell softly eased back into Maria's nose.

"This was my favourite thing to do with auntie Jeanie," she reminisced. She sighed deeply as she surveyed the long swath of grass that lined the ditch. "Come down here. Try not to get your feet wet." Kathy stepped across the thin, shallow pool at the lowest point of the man-made crevasse and Maria followed. From the other side, she squatted and pinched three of the long blades at the base, careful not to upset the roots. She stood up to show her niece.

"This is Mother Earth's hair," she explained. "It's also strong medicine. We smudge with it. We also keep braids of it close by for protection." Maria glanced back over to the van to see the braid hanging in the rearview mirror. "Here, I'll show you how easy it is to braid." She handed Maria the ends of the three long strands. "Pinch these together." Maria held them tied between her thumb and index finger.

Kathy weaved a tiny braid with the three pieces of sweetgrass. She spoke as she braided. "We braid our hair—and our *wiingashk*—for strength. One represents the mind. One represents the body. And one represents the spirit. All three need to be in harmony to live in a good way." In mere seconds, each woman was holding the end of a thin, green braid, about half a metre in length. Kathy took the other end from Maria and pulled her left arm forward. She wrapped the thin weave around her wrist three times and tied it loosely. The smooth grass caressed Maria's thin brown arm. Kathy smiled as she squeezed it tightly, as if to assure her niece that she was there to protect her, and so were the old ways.

"Let's pick some," she said excitedly. They both lowered themselves to the base of the long grass and Kathy showed Maria exactly where to pick the blades to ensure they grow back just as long. They continued until they had two large handfuls each, then walked back to the van and laid them out on the back. "I'll take these home, and we can braid them later," Kathy said. She shut the gate, and they got in their respective driver and passenger sides of the minivan.

Kathy turned the keys to the ignition, and the clock in the console lit up, glowing "11:17". "I think that's enough for today," she said. "That's a lot for you to remember."

"Well *miigwech* auntie," Maria said. "I really liked that. I never knew any of that stuff. If I did, I forgot it a long time ago."

"We'll do this again soon. There's lots more to show you. If you wanna come over tomorrow we'll clean the cedar and sweetgrass."

"Okay, that sounds like a plan."

The ride up had been a bit foreboding, and now that the mood was lighter, Kathy decided to turn on the radio. She pushed the power knob and the Tragically Hip's "Courage" came loudly over the speakers. She cringed and scrambled to turn it down. "Holay!" shouted Maria. "Were you and uncle rockin' this van last night or what?" She laughed.

Kathy rolled her eyes and smiled, and put the minivan into gear. She started a three-point turn on the road to head back down to the highway. The ride back to the rez was a jovial one, filled with jokes and gossip. There was never a chill of awkwardness between the two, but both felt as if a heavy burden of sorrow was lightening on their shoulders. The medicine they gathered made them stronger—Maria especially.

The radio played at a steady volume, and the laughter from the aunt and niece easily drowned it out. They talked about the softball tournament coming up and how that would bring all types out of the woodwork.

"Those Anishinaabe men from down south are shorter than we are up here," noted Kathy, "but they sure got nice bums!"

"Holay, they're young enough to be your sons!" stated Maria.

"Well, I can still look anyways. These men up here don't got bums!"

"There's gonna be a lot of women looking, that's for sure."

They laughed in unison. The tournament was a big deal for both the ballplayers and the women in the community. The latter wanted to see the male specimens other reserves had to offer, and showed up to all the games in teased or permed hair and tight jeans. They joked about what certain notorious women in the community would be wearing. "Your grandmother would send us right to church if she saw us in shorts that short!" said Kathy.

They went on to talk about the upcoming powwow. Birchbark hadn't hosted a traditional gathering of any kind for as long as anyone could remember. The Indian Act banned ceremonial dancing back in the 1920s. The drum hadn't sounded in the open in their community since. But a handful of young men—including Edgar—had been learning the old songs in recent years, and a man named Merle from a rez down south on Georgian Bay gifted them a grandfather drum just a year before. He promised to bring his community's drum up for the powwow too. It wouldn't be a huge gathering like the one in Wikwemikong (commonly known as "Wiky"), but it was a start, and a lot of people were very excited. Maria planned to volunteer for the whole thing.

Kathy turned right onto the road into Birchbark and headed down into the community. They opened the windows, allowing the mild air to flow through the front of the van. It was still too early for lunch so they decided to go up to Henry's for supper the next day instead.

By now there was other traffic on the dusty route. Cars, trucks, and vans passed them on the way to town to buy groceries and run other weekend errands. Kids rode their bikes in either direction. Given the growing heat, some were on the way to the lake to take the first swim of the season. It wouldn't be warm or enjoyable, but it would be a feat of strength for bragging rights.

The van didn't slow as it approached the road leading to the Gibson's house. Instead, Kathy just kept going straight on the main road to the beach. Puzzled, Maria didn't say anything. It was only a few hundred metres beyond her driveway, and soon Kathy was pulling up to the gravel parking lot. She drove directly in and parked the car. She turned off the ignition and the ambient noise of spring on the Great Lakes gently washed over them.

Maria looked at Kathy, then out to the water. It rippled slightly, the deep blue glistening as the sun penetrated the ancient, sacred element. There were fresh footprints in the sand, but there was no one else there. They both expected the kids on bikes to show up shortly.

"Your mom told me she used to take you girls here all the time in the summer," Kathy said, staring straight ahead. Maria wasn't ready to take another difficult trip down memory lane, but she obliged. "Yeah, Eva taught me how to build sandcastles. That's about all I remember."

"I know we talked about a lot today, and I don't want to leave you sad."

Maria nodded silently.

"But there's a reason your mom took you girls down here. She might not have known it at the time. But I think deep down she was getting you ready." Confused, Maria looked at her. Kathy's eyes were intense.

"When you're an *Anishinaabekwe*, you're a keeper of the water. It's called *biish*, or *nbi* in our language. Water is the life-blood of Mother Earth. We carry and give life just as she does. So it's our responsibility to watch it. We have a special bond with it. Your mom was trying to give you that knowledge, even though she didn't have to say anything."

Memories of Clara's smiling face with the powerful blue waves behind her flashed in Maria's mind. They were her favourite images of her mother.

Kathy continued: "The two most important women in your life were taken from you in a violent way. There's nothing you could have done about it. But that has damaged you. It's *not* your fault." She felt the need to repeat this. "*Nobody* knows how to deal with that."

Maria felt the tears coming back.

"And that's what people remember about them; especially your sister. Despite all the good things she did in her young life, her tragedy is her legacy. She'll always be remembered as the victim. And she can't control that. That's the saddest part. And now, your family will always be known for tragedy. That's not fair to any of you."

Maria looked back to the water as tears ran down her cheeks again.

"But you can change that. I can help you. This water is part of that. When you're ready, I can teach you more. It's a lot to take in, but your brother Ed is on his way too. Don't be scared to ask him about the traditional ways—how the body, mind and spirit come together. It has a lot to do with the braid I showed you.

"I'm sorry to make this painful again, but if we don't recognize that pain, we can't heal. We can't redefine our stories. Our legacies live on much longer than we do. So it's up to us to make sure sadness and violence don't define us."

Maria thought about all the time she had been wasting drinking and partying and trying to ignore that persistent, painful buzz of anger and sadness. She understood what her aunt was saying.

"Okay auntie," she said. "*Miigwech.*"

"Come here," Kathy said as she moved in for another close, strong embrace. This one felt better than the last for Maria. She wiped her eyes again. "I'll take you home now, my girl."

Kathy started the van. She backed up and then pulled out of the beach parking lot, heading back north to take a right down the road to the Gibson's. She swerved in and parked the car again, this time leaving the engine running.

"So do you wanna come over tomorrow and clean that cedar and sweetgrass?" she asked.

"Yeah," Maria nodded.

"Okay I'll call you when I'm ready."

"Okay."

"Smile my girl, you're beautiful and the world needs to see that."

Maria smiled and opened the passenger door. She stepped out and made her way back up the steps. She turned around as Kathy backed up, waving on her way out. The grey minivan turned back on to the road and her aunt headed home.

Maria sat down again and pulled out her pack of cigarettes. She pushed it up from the bottom and singled one out. She took a deep breath before grabbing it and placing it subtly between her thin lips. She flicked the red lighter, lit the smoke, and inhaled deeply. As she exhaled, she stared straight into the thick trees and brush in front of her. The emotional purge had left her exhausted. But it gave way for something else.

NORMAN
Fall 1995

Norman grabbed his beer by the neck and tipped it into his mouth while leaning forward on the bar. His denim-clad arms propped up his tall, lean frame, although his shoulders slouched, making the shadow of the beak of his cap conceal the dark circles under his brown eyes. Only his nose and goatee were visible under the overhead light, while his shaggy hair jutted out from under the cap and over his ears like wings.

He put the bottle back down on the finished oak of the bar with more force than he intended. It made a sharp knocking noise that caught the bartender's attention. He turned right from the till where he was making change for an order. "Everything alright, boss?" he asked, with a discerning look and a crooked brow. "Yeah, I'm good," replied Norman. He looked down at his beer and noticed it was already three quarters finished. "Actually I better get another one," he added.

"Sure thing," the bartender uttered as he leaned over to get a cold bottle out of the refrigerator below the register. He walked it over and placed it gently between Norman's nearly-finished beer and the steadily-filling ashtray. Norman handed him two loonies and two quarters. He noticed sweat stains in the armpits of his blue Toronto Maple Leafs t-shirt and beads of perspiration on his pale forehead under his short brown hair. As usual, it was going to be a busy night for the bartender. Norman struggled to remember his name. "Thanks man," is all he could muster.

Steve, the bartender, didn't offer to run a tab for Norman because he was unsure if he'd actually stick around to pay it. He generally didn't run tabs for Natives and figured he'd have to get one of the bouncers to kick Norman out eventually anyway. Although the Ojibways and the whites shared drinks here, there was a subtle, underlying racism that often led to trouble, especially on a Friday or Saturday night. It was an unpredictable bomb that could go off at any moment.

Norman pulled another cigarette from his depleting pack and brought it to his lips. He breathed deeply through his nose before lighting the tobacco. The smoke lifted steadily in a blue-grey stream from the end of his cigarette, augmenting the thick haze that floated just above the heads of the bar patrons. The music seemed to get louder as more and more people gradually came through the Roadhouse. It was a Friday night in Sudbury, and the chilly late November air sneaked in with each new reveller. Mostly men came in groups at first, either having just finished their shifts at the mine or other construction projects around the city. If they didn't work, like Norman, they were there to get an early start on the weekend.

As the lone Ojibway sitting at the bar, Norman was waiting for his buddies Matt Duchesne and Chris Deer. Matt was from a rez just outside the Soo, and Chris came from an Iroquois reserve somewhere down south. They were both there working in the nickel mine. A few attempts to get Norman on their crew failed due mostly to the large gaps of real work on his résumé. He also didn't have his high school diploma. Still, he was able to get random construction jobs from time to time, usually under the table.

Norman collected Unemployment Insurance from a labour job he had with a major construction company that did a lot of the road and highway work in the Sudbury area. He put in his nine months to qualify, and was laid off soon after. He would have been fired for showing up still reeking of alcohol one particular Friday morning, but his supervisor Rick, liked him and worked out an agreement with his manager to make it officially a layoff. Rick was from Waverley and knew the Gibson family's story. It was a rare moment of someone in a position of authority taking pity on a drunken Indian.

He took a swig of the new, cold beer and Creedence Clearwater Revival's "Commotion" came on the jukebox. The Roadhouse owner was too cheap to hire a DJ on the weekends, and he knew people weren't filling his bar for the music or the ambience. They were there for the cheap beer and the easy (and sometimes volatile) company. As such, the jukebox was stuck in a bygone era, and staff just left it on shuffle from open to close most nights of the week. Sometimes traveling cover bands booked gigs here, but that was usually only during the warmer months, erupting in mayhem whenever it happened. Something about live covers of AC/DC and the Tragically Hip really fired up the regulars, and it usually led to a of broken glass and black eyes by the end of the night. But now that winter was just around the corner, anyone who spent more than one night a week at the Roadhouse was bound to hear the same Bob Seger, Janis Joplin, Led Zeppelin, and Creedance Clearwater Revival songs over and over again.

Norman pinched another cigarette out of his pack and shoved it between his lips. He felt himself getting buzzed so he wanted to slow his pace with a smoke. It was a counter-productive move, as the two went hand-in-hand. Every drag was washed down with beer, and every hard gulp was soothed with a long draw on the end of the butt. He went to light it when he felt a hard slap on the back of his faded denim jacket. "Hey Indian, you can't fuckin' smoke here!" He recognized Matt's voice and turned around to see him and Chris standing there. They both smelled of cheap cologne. Chris was even wearing a blue-and-white striped button up shirt tucked neatly into his jeans.

"Holy shit, you Indians lookin' to snag tonight or what?" Norman chuckled as he eyed both of his buddies up and down. They were clearly dressed to impress.

"It's Friday night, man!" asserted Chris. "Gotta look good!"

"Yeah, it's Friday night in Sudbury! All you need to snag here is enough money to buy her a couple beers and shots and cab fare home," said Norman. "That's why I always keep six bucks in my sock, just in case!"

The three of them laughed. "Let's get some beers and go grab that table," said Matt, pointing with his bottom lip to the corner of the room. Chris paid for six bottles—two each so they wouldn't have to get up and order more too soon. Norman downed the rest of the one he had on the bar, put his smoke back in his mouth, and grabbed new, cold bottles in each hand. Matt led the way to the back.

The bar was already pretty full. They maneuvered their way through tables full of middle-aged white people, young white people, young Native people, and the occasional mix of both. By this point the male-female ratio in the bar had evened out, and that was evident with the potent scents of perfume that competed for air space with the cigarette smoke.

Despite their visual differences, the people who frequented the Roadhouse really weren't that different. At least eight reserves—mostly Anishinaabe, or Ojibway—were within an hour's drive of Sudbury. The treaties (the Robinson-Huron Treaty being the predominant one) put most of those communities near small towns and other non-Native settlements nearly a century and a half before. For this stretch of northern Ontario, Sudbury was indeed the "big city", and it's where a lot of people from those reserves and towns migrated to in order to find work, an education, or simply to escape. So for the most part, these cultures were not foreign to each other.

The three Ojibway men put their bottles down on the two low, blacktop tables side-by-side and pulled out the steel-framed chairs with thin cushions covered by torn and blistering black vinyl. Chris and Matt sat with their backs to the wall, facing the rest of the bar, so they could better scope out the scene and snag the hottest prospects, while Norman sat across unburdened and oblivious.

Technically, Norman still had a girlfriend, so he chose to keep his wandering eyes away from potential temptations. He wasn't certain if Denise was going to show up at the Roadhouse later on in the night. She mentioned it to him earlier in the day. But their relationship was a volatile one at best—mostly due to his financial uncertainty and occasional emotional absence - so he figured it really could go either way. Regardless, he mentally prepared himself to see her so his initial strategy was to be on his best behaviour. For a while, anyway.

Matt seemed to read his mind. "What's Denise up to tonight?" he asked.

"I dunno," Norman replied. "I haven't seen her since before she went to work this morning. I think she's coming out later."

"Are you guys still together?"

"She hasn't kicked me out yet. I'm still crashing at her place."

"You guys getting along?"

"I guess you could call it that. No big scraps lately anyways."

"Sounds like you're due for some trouble!" Matt nudged

Chris with his elbow. "Let's get some shots!"

Norman smiled uneasily and shook his head. "Fuckin' guys!" he muttered as he took off his hat momentarily to run his fingers through his dark, greasy hair. "You're gonna get me thrown in the fuckin' doghouse."

"You're already pretty much there buddy," Chris laughed. He got up and walked to the bar. He was soon back with a tray of six shots of Jack Daniels in small, heavy one-ounce glasses. He passed two across to Norman and two to Matt at his left. He sat down and pulled his chair close to the table. Matt rubbed his hands quickly together as if to warm them. "Alright, what are we drinking to?" he asked.

"To Normy's new single life!" bellowed Chris.

"Fuck off!" Norman protested.

"Ok then, to the doghouse! Because we all need to stay there once in a while."

"Alright then, to the doghouse!" said Matt with a smile.

"To the doghouse," reluctantly echoed Norman.

They knocked the tiny glasses together and looked each other in the eyes. They each tipped their heads back and dumped the whiskey down their throats. It soothed Norman's already smoke-worn gullet. He felt its warmth illuminate his insides as gravity pulled the liquor down to his gut. The three men slammed the glasses back down on the table simultaneously. They looked at each other again before downing the next one. Norman noticed Chris' eyes watering, and Matt gave out a slight cough.

"To Uncle Jack, who's tasting great tonight," declared Norman.

"To Uncle Jack," repeated the other two.

The second shot went down just as smoothly for Norman, and much more easily for Chris and Matt. Norman was a few beers ahead of the other two, so the pacifying blanket of alcohol was already draped lightly over his shoulders.

Suspended in early intoxication is where Norman felt best. The alcohol helped him focus on the moment and the pseudo-happiness. It had him in its grip in this early stage of drunkenness, and as usual, Norman naively believed he had control and could steer his emotions with the booze. But maintaining this equilibrium of temporary joy, false hope, and tenuous restraint always required more beer and whiskey, and that's where things started to get shaky.

Still, here he was, enjoying a Friday night at the bar with his friends. They discussed a wide range of things, from the Leafs to the politics of their respective reserves to the rumours swirling around the potential sale of the nickel mine in Sudbury. As mundane as these conversations were, the words and sentiments were easy distractions from Norman's ongoing troubles. His unemployment. His troubled romantic life. His perpetual unsettled feelings attached to the tragedies in his family life that dictated the relationships within it. His addiction to alcohol and his occasional abuse of drugs.

"I think I'm gonna drive home, not next weekend but the weekend after," said Matt, out of the blue. "Wanna ride?"

Birchbark was on the way to Matt's rez along Highway 17. It was an easy way home if Norman needed it. He didn't bother going with him at Thanksgiving because he wasn't up for facing his older brother with nothing really new to report: no job, unstable relationship, alcoholism. He thought about it quickly and realized he hadn't been home at all the previous summer. "Maybe," Norman replied. "Guess I should check on my brothers and my little sister."

It had been so long since he called Edgar that he was unaware Stanley just graduated with his Bachelor's degree the previous spring and was going back to University in Ottawa for a Master's. Maria, meanwhile, had enrolled in a Social Work diploma course at a college in the Soo. The only sibling he had left in Birchbark was his older brother Edgar. They lived two very different lives and thus rarely talked. They joked and behaved cordially when together, as brothers always do, but outside of those visits they had very little in common. In a superficial way, Norman resented his brother just because he lived a positive and clean life. He couldn't help but feel inferior.

Matt's question was like a sledgehammer blow to the emotional wall Norman had cemented together that night with the fragile compound of booze. It left an aggravating crack that threatened to spread with each thought of home. These thoughts were like a drill, poking holes in that barrier with a persistent buzz that became increasingly harder to ignore. The whole façade was doomed to collapse, and unravel into a tattered, dirty heap of violence, abuse, and depravity.

A steady succession of drinks fast-forwarded the evening beyond the cordial, casual, and civilized discussions, and before long the three men in their late-twenties were nearly fall-down drunk. Casual acquaintances and other random bar-goers joined them at their table at various points throughout the night. Most of them were Matt and Chris' co-workers from the mine and their friends. Others were fellow bar regulars, whom the three came to recognize and know through somewhat regular visits to the Roadhouse in recent years. Most of them knew Matt and Chris by name, but few remembered Norman. He preferred it that way.

Norman got up to go visit the urinal. He was mindful of his feet, making sure he didn't stumble. That would surely draw the eyes of Steve and the bouncers. The latter were no doubt eager by this point of the night to manhandle someone out of the bar—preferably an Indian. Testosterone was simmering and it needed some kind of release. Nonetheless, Norman concentrated on the task at hand and was in and out of the bathroom in a typically sober amount of time.

As he walked back to the table, he noticed two women sitting across from his buddies. One was in his seat, so he grabbed an empty chair from a nearby table, pulled it up to the side, and collapsed into it. He looked through glossy eyes at the two white brunettes across from Matt and Chris.

"This is our buddy Norm," said Matt. "He's a living legend!"

"Hi Norm!" the two said in unison, introducing themselves as Jen and Jess.

"Jen and Jessss?" Norman slurred. "You guys twins?"

They giggled. "We get that all the time," said the one farthest from him. He already forgot which one she was, Jen or Jess.

They had similar straight, mid-length hairstyles. The one closest to him—Jess—reeked of potent perfume that seemed to congest his nose. He assumed she must have doused her tight, button-up flannel shirt in it. The shirt was undone to her cleavage, and she caught Norman's slow-motion eyes peeking down into the accentuated milky-white crevasse. His drunken glance became a fixated gaze, but it didn't faze her. She was focused on Chris, who was sitting directly across.

The five of them carried on inane drunken banter—the kind that seems profound at the time, but to hear a recording of it with sober ears would be nothing short of embarrassing. Matt and Chris talked about work. Jen and Jess disclosed they came from Lively, a town just outside of Sudbury. Norman joined in when the conversation came around to rez life. And the voices kept spiralling, landing on simple themes like sports, music, and basic local politics. It was all irrelevant though because the white women coveted the Native men—Matt with his shaved head that made his neck and shoulders look huge in his black Stone Temple Pilots t-shirt, and Chris in his business-casual shirt and short, gelled hair—and this banter was a mere prelude to a different kind of dance. Norman just watched, drunkenly amused by the eyes the women were making at his buddies and the ridiculous stories they told to try to impress them.

Led Zeppelin's "Ramble On" resounded from the jukebox and Matt responded with a loud "Fuckin right!" before strumming on an air guitar. Chris rolled his intoxicated eyes slowly and said "Every fuckin' time! When they gonna update the tunes in here? My dad used to play this shit way too much when I was a kid."

"These are the Classics, dumbass!"

"I don't give a shit! I've heard this song so many times—especially here—that I could play it off by heart. And I don't even know how to play fuckin' guitar!"

Chris let out a sharp cackle and turned to each of them, as if seeking approval. He then leaned far over the table, and with his destabilized equilibrium knocked over one of Matt's beers with his elbow. The women laughed and Norman just chuckled.

"Lord of the Rings!" Norman proclaimed, thrusting his beer in the air.

"Huh?" asked Chris.

"Lord of the Rings!" Jen and Jess looked at him, puzzled but laughing.

"What in the fuck are you talking about, Indian?"

"This song's about Lord of the fuckin' Rings. Listen to the lyrics!"

The bad audio mix of the jukebox amplified by the bar's P.A. punched up the bass and guitar and drowned out Robert Plant's vocals. "I can't hear shit, man!" Yelled Matt.

Norman explained. "He's singing about Gollum and Mordor and shit like that. That's from Lord of the Rings. My little bro Stan told me all about that."

"What's Lord of the Rings?" asked Jen.

Norman decided just to let it go and the conversation carried on. Then he noticed Chris look up at someone behind him. His smiling face hardened slightly. Norman turned to his right and saw two white guys in jeans and tight shirts hovering over Jen and Jess. All Norman could focus on was their moustaches.

"Well good evening Jess," said the one on the right with the blonde mullet.

Her response wasn't as friendly: "What do you want, Randy?"

"Just saying hi," he said defensively and sarcastically, putting his palms up before clenching them into fists. "Can't an old friend come over and say hi?"

The immediate tension was slightly sobering, and even in his drunken haze, Norman could tell these two were most likely exes with a tumultuous past.

"Who are your friends here?" Randy asked. His nameless buddy standing beside him turned and nodded at someone else across the room. Norman knew what was about to happen. Seeing as he, Matt and Chris were three and the unexpected guests were two, they were calling in reinforcement.

"It doesn't matter who they are Randy," said Jen loudly. "Just leave Jess alone. It's over between you two!"

Norman looked at Jess as she stared sheepishly down at the table with her bottom lip quivering. He glanced over at his friends, who were on the edge of their seats, ready to spring into action.

"It's none of your business, Jen," Randy responded sternly. "But come on—tell me you're both not fucking these Indians!"

Sharp squeaks came from the chair legs rubbing on the linoleum floor before they knocked heavily into the back wall as Matt and Chris instantly stood up. "What the fuck did you say, white boy?" said Matt through gritted teeth. Norman cautiously got to his feet, as he noticed a third shorter man pacing quickly towards them.

Randy looked right into Matt's eyes. "I said you keep your diseased red dicks away from these women or we'll cut 'em off," he said.

Chris took a deep breath. "Alright," he said calmly. "You fuckheads got a couple seconds to turn around and get the fuck outta here. Or else we're gonna fuck you up."

The two women frantically tried to ease the situation that was getting rapidly out of hand. They held up their arms between the two groups and begged for peace and order. Norman sized up the third man that had entered the scenario and knew he'd be no match. He looked scared. Still, he plotted his moves in his mind anyway. A quick jab with the left always catches them off guard, because in bar fights tough guys are always throwing and waiting for the big haymaking right hand. Unless he was left-handed, of course. He had a combination of punches in mind and if that didn't work, he'd just shoot in with a double-leg take down. Norman was on the wrestling team in high school before he dropped out in grade 10.

Almost as if they orchestrated it, Norman took a quick step to his right while Chris picked up the table with both hands and heaved it to his side. He stepped forward with a hard right straight to Randy's nose. It seemed to explode in a bloody fountain, but he stayed on his feet and started swinging back immediately. Jen and Jess screamed as they scrambled out of the way. Matt squared off with the nameless buddy and grabbed him by the shoulders before head-butting him. Norman knew this was his cue, so he turned to the third brawler and quickly jabbed him in the nose with a left before swinging wide with a right, connecting with his jaw right below the ear. His legs crumpled and he fell to the floor, out cold.

The already barbaric ambience of the bar got even more vicious. Women screamed while other men stood on chairs to watch. Bottles and glasses shattered on the floor in the melee. In the adrenaline rush, Norman didn't see Chris knock out Randy, and in a few seconds, bouncers had rushed in to break up Matt and the other thug, who were exchanging blows. He looked to the floor to see Randy's legs twitching. He could hear him snoring beneath the music and the shouting. Directly across from him, Jen consoled Jess as she sobbed. His head then jerked sideways as a bouncer grabbed the shoulders of his jean jacket and proceeded to haul him out of the bar. The other two bouncers wrestled with Chris and Matt and forced them across the room as well, before throwing all three out into the cold November night. "Hey, my fuckin' jacket is still in there!" Chris protested on the way out. "I don't give a shit," was the only response.

Once they were outside, the three regrouped and turned to the security staff. A bouncer with a shaved bald white head and Harley-Davidson t-shirt stared them down, panting heavily and trembling with rage. "Get the fuck out of here!" He shouted. "Or we're gonna call the cops!"

"Look what that motherfucker did to my shirt!" shouted Chris, pulling open the wide rip in the shoulder of his shirt. "I need my jacket!"

"Fuck it man, let's just go," said Matt. "I got beer at my house and I can give you a shirt. It's only 11, lots of action still happening tonight."

Chris shook his head in drunken disgust at the security staff and turned to walk down the street. Matt's apartment was only a few blocks away, and that was only a few more blocks from downtown. They decided to clean up and try their luck at the clubs down there. The night was young, and they could still walk. Once they got around the corner from the Roadhouse, Matt took a piss while Norman leaned over to puke. They got to Matt's within minutes, cracked open more beers, and that's the last memory Norman had from that night.

Norman woke up to a bright fluorescent light shining directly in his face. He was conscious, but his eyes were closed and all he could see was red as his eyelids futilely filtered the unnatural light. His mouth was dry and he couldn't breathe through his nose. He was lying on his back on a hard surface and his back was sore. Stark chatter came from a hallway close by, but he couldn't make out the words. He moved to turn to his side without opening up his eyes. He knew the piercing light would be painful.

Although he couldn't smell or see, he had a pretty good idea where he was. He had woken up here a handful of times before. He wasn't ready to let on to the cops that he was awake yet, so he jogged his painfully foggy memory from the night before to try to remember how exactly he got thrown in the drunk tank. All he remembered was knocking out a white guy then doing shots at Matt's apartment. There was a dark, strange, and likely dangerous and embarrassing void between there and here. He wasn't sure if he was ready to hear about it yet. Either way, he'd have to call Denise to pay to get him out of the cop shop, and that was certain to be an ugly discussion.

One of the constables knocked his club against the side of the cell with a sharp "clang". "Rise and shine sweetie!" he chirped. Norman slowly opened his eyes and let them adjust to the throbbing white luminescence of the room before responding. His head pounded and he was thirsty. He took another deep breath through his mouth and propped himself up on his right elbow. He squinted in the direction of the hall, and saw a tall figure in a dark blue uniform standing there, stereotypically slapping the club in the palm of his hand like a jail guard from the movies.

"Jesus Norm, you look like shit!" said the officer. Norman recognized his voice and his sarcastic, joking demeanour. He sat all the way up on the concrete slab and put his feet flat on the floor. It felt cold through his socks. He looked down at himself. His t-shirt was caked stiff with blood, and there were purple stains all over the thighs of his jeans, where the blood soaked into the blue denim. Because he couldn't inhale through his nostrils, he had a pretty good idea all that blood came from his nose. He turned his head back to the hall.

"I've been better," he admitted.

"Well from what I heard you and the boys had a pretty wild night. I was wondering when you'd turn up again. I haven't seen you in a while!"

Norman recognized the officer's voice. He tried to remember him. It had been at least a month since he woke up in the drunk tank. It wasn't as if he was purposely trying to stay away, he just usually passed out before there was an opportunity to get into any real trouble. "Well officer..." he began.

"Constable Dawson," the cop interrupted.

"Constable Dawson," Norman continued. "You win some, you lose some. Not sure what I lost last night. I guess I'll find out today."

"You got the same old lady?"

"Yeah."

Dawson clenched his teeth and inhaled sharply through them, the universal expression for bracing for trouble. "Yikes," he said.

"Think I could get a shower?"

"Nah, sorry Norm. We're not allowed to do that. You're gonna have to suck it up again. Might do ya some good to get knocked down a couple notches by the old lady."

Norman couldn't dispute that.

"I'll give ya a couple more minutes to shake out the cobwebs, then we gotta get you outta here. Can't be in here longer than 8AM"

"Alright, thank you, sir."

Dawson walked out of sight and back to the desk. Norman leaned forward and put his head in his hands. His hat was gone and his hair was so greasy it almost felt wet. He couldn't remember the last time he had a shower. Otherwise the rest of his clothes were in tact, save for the blood stains. He gritted his teeth and brought his right thumb and forefinger up to the bridge of his nose. Gently and slowly, he squeezed it, and pain shot though his face like sharp electrical currents. It didn't feel swollen, though, so he doubted that it was broken. He didn't remember taking a hit during the brawl at the Roadhouse. This must have happened sometime after. For all he knew, it could have been one of the cops that threw him in the drunk tank. Either way, he knew he probably looked terrible, and Denise would not be impressed. There was no guarantee that she would pick him up anyway.

He stood up to stretch, and Dawson was back at the bars to slide them open. "Let's go, buddy," he said. "It's checkout time at Chez Sudbury Police." Norman still felt drunk and still likely was, legally. In reality, it had only been five and a half hours since the police picked him up outside of the Academy night-club on Elgin Street. He had passed out alone on the sidewalk. The young officers on duty roused him, and he became agitated. They tried to subdue him, and he resisted. As a result, one of the arresting officers slammed him face-first into the hood of the cruiser and held him down as the other handcuffed him behind his back. A red pool of blood outlining his face was left on the white hood when they lifted him off the car to throw him in the back.

Norman stepped out of the cell and followed Dawson down the hall to get processed out. The lights were annoyingly bright throughout the cellblock, forcing him to squint as he shuffled through. He didn't notice anyone else being held there. He looked around on the off-chance that Chris and Matt were picked up along with him, but he knew that was highly unlikely. They rarely went to the drinking extremes that he did. They had a lot more to lose. Compared to them, Norman was just another jobless, high-school dropout from the rez who was defined by those who knew him only by his family's tragedies. He had made little effort in his adult life to rewrite that definition. Instead, his priority was finding ways to get money as easily as possible to get drunk and forget about everything bad that happened to him. He knew that he was a twenty-eight-year-old stereotype and a statistic who blamed everyone else for his lamentable situation.

He approached the desk at the end of the hall. The grey-haired officer sitting behind it took off his wide-rimmed glasses to reveal an angry brow. "I hope you slept off that shitty attitude," he deadpanned. The statement caught Norman off guard. "Uh ..." he paused, unsure how to respond.

"We could have charged you with resisting arrest and assaulting a police officer," the veteran cop warned Norman. "You'd be on your way to remand now, instead of checking out of here."

Norman was silent. He only nodded.

"Fact is you may have been more at home there with your kind. Seems to be a lot of you guys ending up in the courts these days. All because of booze. But we haven't seen you here for a while. Figured you were getting your shit together. So consider this your last get out of jail free card."

Norman cleared his throat. "Thank you sir," he responded, ignoring the racism and wanting to get this awkward ritual over with as soon as possible. "But if your drunk ass ends up here again," the officer went on, "you'll be charged, mark my word. You fuckin' Indians can't seem to get off the bottle! Jesus Christ."

He grabbed an open plastic white box to his left and lifted it up to the front counter. Norman's jean jacket and Doc Martens boots were inside, along with his scant wallet. His hat was missing. "Was there a Yankees hat in here?" he asked.

"Don't push your luck, Gibson," the officer behind the desk said flatly. Just grab your shit and go call whoever the fuck is gonna spring to get your drunk ass out of here."

Norman turned to Dawson, who just raised his eyebrows and shrugged. He grabbed his possessions from the box, and Dawson motioned him towards the phone at a small desk against the wall beside him. Norman's mouth opened to take another deep breath, and he walked over and sat down at the stool. He leaned over to put on his boots before making the call. They were the most expensive items he owned.

After tying the red laces tight, he sat up and turned to the office phone. He remembered from his last stay here that he had to dial "9" before the number. He punched in the seven digits and listened for the ring tone. It rang four times before a light click broke the steady rhythm of hums. It took a couple of seconds before a groggy "hello?" was heard from the other end of the line.

Norman swallowed hard. "Hey, it's me."

"Norm?"

"Yeah."

"Where are you? I thought we were supposed to meet at the Roadhouse last night!"

"I got kicked outta there."

"Jesus Christ. What did you do?"

"We got into a fight."

"Well where did you go then?"

"We went to Matt's for a bit. I didn't see none of your friends there so I couldn't let you know."

"Jesus. So why are you calling me now?"

"I'm at the cop shop. I woke up in the drunk tank."

He heard a deep sigh on the other end. "Fuck sakes."

"Can you come and pay my fine? I'll pay you back on Thursday."

"It's early!"

"I know, but they're kicking me outta here."

The frustration and disappointment was easily audible through the phone line.

"Fuck. Okay, I'll be there in fifteen minutes."

"Okay thanks babe. I'm just gonna warn you though—I don't look good."

"You never look good these days Norm."

He heard a sharp click and the phone went silent. "K, see ya," he said to no one, before slowly placing the phone on the receiver. He thanked Dawson and got up and moved to the chair by the heavily fortified door.

In fifteen minutes, Denise walked up to the bulletproof glass-shielded front desk and didn't bother to look in his direction. Norman could only see her head and shoulders. Her hair was tied back tightly into a ponytail, and wide sunglasses concealed what she was feeling.

She paid his fine and turned quickly to head back out the front doors to her white sedan parked out on the street. The officer buzzed him out, and he slowly and shamefully followed her outside. The sun wasn't even above the low skyline of the northern metropolis yet. He walked down the concrete stairs and slunk in the passenger side of her car. She stared straight ahead, armoured in her black leather jacket and dark glasses.

Norman felt the tension and awkwardness in the ride back to her apartment. The drive was slow and silent. They pulled up to her three-story brick building in the Copper Cliff neighbourhood of the city. Denise turned off the car without saying anything and headed for the front door. Norman followed up the stairs to her third-floor pad. She unlocked the door and threw the keys in a bowl on a table by the entrance. "You look and smell like shit," she said without turning to him. "You better take a shower."

Norman stepped into the apartment and leaned over to untie his boots. He stepped on the heel of each with either foot to shove them off. Then took off his jacket and hung it on the hook above the table with the bowl of keys. Denise was at the sink rinsing out a green plastic cup to fill with cold water. The kitchen table in front of her was littered with a dozen or so beer bottles, empty cigarette packs, and a couple of overflowing ashtrays. "Looks like you guys had a good night too," Norman quipped. She ignored him.

He walked across the stained yellow carpet past the kitchen on the left and living room on the right. There were even more brown bottles and plastic cups on the coffee table. The sliding door to the balcony was wide open, airing out the stale boozy, smoky apartment with the late November chill. The sun was now peeking above the other apartment buildings to the east and shone brightly onto the yellow, grey, and brown floor. Denise turned around to face the rest of the apartment while drinking her water. Norman stepped into the bathroom down the hallway and closed the door.

He reached into the shower and let it run as he took his clothes off. His shirt and jeans were stained with blood, dirt, booze, and probably piss. He couldn't smell it, but he knew that sometimes when he passed out that drunk, he lost all control of his bladder. He figured Dawson would have told him if he pissed himself. He seems like a pretty decent guy, Norman thought. He must have grown up around Indians, or his parents are social workers or something. Either way, he didn't seem racist to Norman.

With his clothes in a heap in the corner by the door, he turned to the mirror. This was always the worst part of the process. He turned around and looked into it. His reflection didn't shock or surprise him. It was just a matter of facing the results of the night before and his ongoing emotional struggles and addictions. His hair was messy, flattened in spots, and shooting out in others. It had a distinct shine thanks to the oil his scalp accumulated after days without shampoo.

He traced the diagonal scrape on his forward down to his still-swollen bloodshot eyes. Dark bruises were already forming underneath them, and by the end of the day he would certainly have a double-shiner. These temporary disfigurements overshadowed his normally deep, brown observant eyes. Unfortunately, he had spent too much time in recent years obscuring that once clear vision.

In between his blackening eyes was his slightly swollen red nose. There was a small cut on the bridge. Thick, dark, crusty clots clogged his nostrils, and streaks of dried blood coated his upper lip. The mirror began to fog over with the thick steam from the hot shower. He turned to draw back the clear vinyl shower curtain, torn from some of the rings that attached it to the rod.

Norman placed one foot into the pooling hot water at the bottom of the tub. It was very hot to the touch, but he still felt a chill from the awkward sleep in the cold drunk tank and needed to warm up. He stepped all the way in and turned his back to the showerhead immediately, gauging the heat with the tougher skin on his back. The water beat heavily on his shoulders in a constant rhythm of soothing heat.

He hung his head and let the steady stream run down his back and his legs. The hot steam enveloped him, relaxing his muscles and easing the tension in his back and shoulders. He turned to face the pulsing water, letting it soak his hair and work the grime and blood from his face. He blew sharply out of his nose and looked down as the dark blood clots swirled into the drain. Blood started pouring from his nose again, creating a red spiral in the clear water churning at the bottom of the porcelain tub. Mesmerized, he stared as the two essential life fluids danced together before descending into the depths of Sudbury's sewage system.

He finished washing, towelled off, and then dressed himself in a clean white t-shirt and jeans he pulled from a pile of clothes on the floor in Denise's room. His head pounded as he sobered up. He walked out to the living room and found her sitting on the couch, staring into a dark TV on the other side of the room and smoking a cigarette. The rising sun on her tired frame created a faint reflection in the curved glass. She wore a blue sweat-shirt and grey sweatpants, and her eye makeup from the evening before was smudged. Norman noticed a just-opened beer on the coffee table in front of her. A thin layer of moisture coated the outside of the bottle, causing it to stand out from the lipstick-stained and fingerprinted others. She picked up the cold, full bottle and tipped it into her mouth.

She put it down firmly back on the coffee table before saying "you gotta go, Norman. I can't do this anymore." It wasn't a shock because he was expecting this anytime. At this point, it was more of an inconvenience than anything. His first thought was where else could he crash in Sudbury? He didn't challenge her, not only because he didn't have the energy, but because he knew he had little chance at any sort of absolution. They had been together for about five months, and he had been staying with her for the last three. She never really invited him to; he just sort of kept his stuff there.

"Okay," he muttered. "Thanks for getting me out today.

Thanks for letting me stay here."

"No problem," she replied. "I just think this will get worse before it gets better."

That could have meant any number of things. A drunken argument could have led to violence. She could end up broke bailing him out and constantly paying for his booze and food. Even more complicated—she could end up pregnant.

"Yeah, gotcha. Mind if I have a beer before I go?"

He needed the time to figure out what he was going to do. The rising sun was now caressing the tops of the brown bottles.

"Yeah go ahead. There are a few left in the fridge."

"*Miigwech.*"

He stepped over to the fridge and grabbed a chilly bottle and twisted off the cap. He took one harsh mouthful of the soothing beer, walked into the living room and sat on the love seat.

"You're a good guy Norm," she said. "You just get too crazy sometimes."

The hair of the dog was in full effect as she took another drink herself. He ignored the hypocrisy of the moment because he knew she had a point. He was drinking a breakfast beer too, so the pot and the kettle shared a peaceful moment of shared self-pity.

Denise went on. "You got some things you gotta deal with. You know what I'm talking about. This isn't the way to do it."

He nodded and stared into the small opening of the bottle. The brown glass lip blurred as his eyes focused on the tiny bubbles settling inside. He couldn't think of anything to say in response to that. "Mind if I have a smoke?"

She motioned her head to the open pack surrounded by empties. He leaned over to pick one out and lit it up. "I think you should probably go home," she said. "Back to Birchbark."

"Alright, fuck, enough," Norman was annoyed. Denise stopped talking and took another drag of her smoke.

"I'm gonna give you some money. Think about it anyways," she said.

Norman stared blankly at the beer in his hands again. He didn't want a handout, but he could really use the cash. "I'll go get my shit together," he said. He leaned over to drop the burning cigarette butt into an empty bottle and got up to go to her room. He shoved the few changes of clothes that were still on the floor into a large gym bag with the rest of his clothes and came back to the living room in under two minutes. He dropped the bag by the door, sat down and reached for his beer, noticing a thin stack of twenty dollar bills beside it.

"That's a hundred bucks," she said. "More than enough to get you on a bus to Waverley. I know you're probably gonna blow some cash again tonight, so I gave you extra to make sure you still have enough for a ticket."

Norman stared at the cash. He needed it. There was no use declining her kind gesture. He looked up at her, pulled in his lips to slightly conceal a grateful smile and nodded. "*Miigwech*," he said. He picked up the five bills, folded them in half, and put them in the right front pocket of his jeans. It was an emotionally awkward moment and they could both sense the unease in each other.

"Or is this to pay me for my services one last time?" Norman smirked, winking at her.

"Fuck off!" she giggled, before picking a bottle cap up off the table and throwing it at him. He dodged it and started laughing along with her. They fell silent and both took another drink, looking in random wayward directions. He gulped back the rest of the beer to accelerate the desensitization and set it softly back on the coffee table.

"Well, I guess I better go," he said, breaking the silence once again. He wasn't sure where he was going, but he was thinking about trying his luck at Matt's for the time being. "Okay," she responded. He stood up, and she got up almost simultaneously and stepped around the coffee table to hug him. They both squeezed tightly. "You take care," she whispered into his ear.

"You too," he said. "Thanks … and sorry for everything."

Their embrace eased and she pulled back to face him. "You'll make a good woman happy someday," she said. "You just gotta get your shit together!" She gave him an affectionate punch in the shoulder. He smiled and broke from her to grab his boots.

The red laces were fading to pink, and the black toes bore more scuff marks after yet another boozed-up escapade. He pulled them on standing up, with Denise watching over him. He tied his boots loosely and stood up to grab his jean jacket.

"Stay outta trouble!" she commanded, as he put one arm after the other into the jacket. "You too!" he said. "See ya later." He opened the door, walked down the stairs and out into the cold November morning. A hint of sulphur taunted his nostrils. He adjusted the shoulder strap of the bag and started walking towards Power Street to try to hail a cab.

Norman looked down at the round, black puck resting on the wide piece of faded plywood on the grass. Brown leaves lay scattered throughout the backyard. His next chore would be raking those up, following this shooting session. He heard the back door of the house open behind him, and turned to see his father Bill walk out, holding his own hockey stick in one hand with his gloves tucked under the arm of his red plaid jacket. He brushed his shaggy black hair from the top of his glasses with his free hand. Norman took a deep breath and turned his attention back to the task at hand.

He gently shoved the puck back and forth on the wood with his own stick, getting the feel of the friction. The flat surface was getting old, but it was still smooth. He looked up at the rusted old net—his target—just a few metres away towards the back of the yard. His padded hockey gloves were dry, stiff, and smelly, and it would take about ten shots to really soften them up. Bill approached and stopped by the bucket of pucks beside the plywood.

"Chilly this morning eh?" he said to his son.

"Yeah, we may as well be in the arena!" Norman replied.

It was mid-fall morning and the Waverley Minor Hockey house league season had just begun. Having just turned twelve, Norman was in his first year of the Peewee age division, and he had aspirations of being selected for the town's traveling team. But both he and his father knew he needed a stronger wrist shot as a right winger. So Norman spent an hour every day practicing his shot at home. On this particular Saturday morning, Bill came out to check on his progress, and to take a few shots himself. He still played in the Old-timers league with a team of some of the older guys from Birchbark.

With his left hand holding the butt of the stick, Norman reached down the shaft with his right hand and gripped firmly. He leaned over slightly to prepare to shoot. His own blue plaid jacket hung loosely over his tight jeans. The sleeves were tucked tightly into the gloves. He eyed the puck through his slanted, dark brown eyes, and tapped it forward gently with the blade of the stick. He brought it back with the outside of the blade, stickhandling a few times before choosing his angle. Although the plywood surface was old, the cold morning hardened the board and seemed to reduce the drag. It wasn't ice, but it would have to do in a rez backyard dozens of kilometres from the rink.

Norman tapped the puck back and forth a few more times, then brought it back quickly behind him to unleash a strong wrist shot. The puck wobbled slightly on release, but straightened out on its way to the net. A loud "ding" echoed through the birch trees as the black disc careened off the rusted right goal post. The net itself wasn't pretty, but when Bill heard Sam the Zamboni driver at the Waverley Arena say he needed to take it to the dump, Bill offered to take it off his hands for free. "The boys will love this," he told Sam, as he helped load it into the back of his truck.

"You're dragging it too much," the father, as lifelong coach, told the son. "Any decent defenceman is gonna knock the puck off your stick before you even get it away."

"Alright," muttered Norman, accepting the pointer.

"You gotta release it quicker."

"Mmmmm hmmmm."

"You been doing those wrist exercises?"

"A little bit." Norman actually hadn't. Bill had tied a five pound weight and a stick together with about a metre of rope. He instructed Norman to turn the stick with his wrists to lift the weight, elevating it with each twist. It usually made his wrists burn painfully in just a couple of reps.

"You should be doing that every morning when you get up," said Bill.

"Okay. Sometimes I forget," replied Norman.

"If you wanna make the traveling team you need a good and fast wristshot."

"Yeah, I know."

"Go on, take a few more."

Bill kicked over the bucket of pucks onto the plywood and Norman shot each of them at the net. His accuracy was improving, but his speed wasn't. Bill stepped onto the board to demonstrate. They alternated until all three dozen or so pucks were in or behind the net. They both walked up to collect them all, and returned to the designated shooting spot to do it all over again. Except for the occasional tip and brief question, the routine repeated mostly in silence.

As they took their positions once again, a truck roared by on the main road and Norman caught a glimpse of what looked like a cab full of hunters. The sight coupled with the smell of the crisp autumn air reminded him of the one time his father took him and Edgar hunting briefly when they were boys. It was an unsuccessful three-hour excursion into the bush on the north side of the highway. There wasn't much memorable about their sole hunting trip, but Norman wondered aloud why they never went back out.

"Hey dad," he broke the silence of the thinning fall atmosphere.

"Yeah?" Bill replied.

"Remember that time we went hunting?"

"Yeah."

Norman shyly looked down at his feet. He raised his head and gave his father a friendly, inquisitive smile from the corner of his mouth. "How come you never took us again?"

It was Bill's turn to look at his feet. He cleared his throat uneasily, before grasping at an attempt at humour to ease the internal awkwardness. "Ah, it's just easier buying steak at the grocery store," he chuckled. "Besides, how boring is it just to walk through the bush for hours, without getting nothing?"

The more Norman jogged his memory the more he disagreed with Bill's defensive statement. He now recalled it as a good bonding experience with his father and his older brother. "Yeah, guess so," Norman lied. He hoped maybe they'd be able to do it again someday.

Without really thinking, he followed that up with another uncomfortable question. "Were the Ojibway people good hunters?"

"Maybe once, a long time ago," replied Bill somewhat easily.

"Why don't we hunt anymore?" asked the twelve-year-old.

"Like I said, we don't need to."

"Ed told me it was part of learning how to be a man a long time ago."

"Yeah, maybe a long time ago," Bill repeated. He took a deep breath and briefly gazed into the bush beyond the net. "We're not like that anymore."

Norman turned his focus back to the pucks and prepared to shoot again.

After a fifteen minute ride with a ten dollar fare, the taxi dropped Norman off in front of Matt's building close to downtown. It was only 9:30AM and he didn't expect his buddy to be awake yet, but he rang the buzzer of the walk-up anyway. The large, converted white house had four apartments, and Matt's was in the basement. There was no answer, so Norman pressed the buzzer again after about a minute. Following a few silent moments, he heard heavy footsteps trudging up the stairs. The door opened to reveal a shirtless, squinting Matt wearing only jeans.

"Holy fuck look what the cat dragged in!" he shouted. "What the hell happened to you last night? You disappeared after we left here. Looks like you got into some shit!"

"I dunno," Norman replied. "But I ended up in the drunk tank."

Matt laughed. "Jesus Christ man, well get in here. We gotta pick up where we left off!"

He turned around to go back down the stairs and Norman followed, closing the wooden front door tightly behind him. They walked into Matt's apartment and Norman quickly shed his outdoor gear and gym bag and collapsed on the couch. He lay there for a second, scanning the Metallica, Alice in Chains, and Pamela Anderson posters on the wall around him. It looked like a teenager's room rather than a grown man's apartment.

Matt called from the kitchen just a few metres away. "Hair of the dog?"

"Already had one," Norman replied, "but sure."

Matt grabbed a can from the fridge and tossed it underhand across the room. Norman caught it and set it on the low, glass table beside him before opening it. This was the most sober he'd felt in the last twenty-four hours. For some reason, he felt like he should savour it for a moment.

"I'm almost out," Matt said. "After a couple of these we should go for a cruise to get a bite then hit the beer store."

"Sounds good." Norman sat upright and reached for the beer. The sharp crack of the can opening was muffled by the damp, booze-and-smoke-laden basement air, and before long, the following hours blurred together in a malignant mix of steady debauchery and apathetic abuse.

It started with that drive to the greasy spoon with open cans of beer in Matt's dark blue pickup truck. By that point they were most likely legally drunk, but the rationale was that the food they were about to eat would set them a little straighter. Then they found out it was late enough for lunch so they ordered guilt-free caesars with their burgers. That quickly turned into two more each, but the escalating bill coerced them out the door and off to the beer store to stock up for the rest of the weekend. After a long lunch comprised mostly of liquids followed by a case of beer, the goodwill funds Norman got from Denise were long-gone.

It continued with a dangerously drunken drive back to Matt's apartment, picking up Chris and other partiers along the way. Somehow Chris managed to track down the two white women from the night before ("What can I say? Sudbury's a small city, boss!" is all he replied when Norman asked *how*). At one point they were in the truck's cab while Chris and Norman shivered in the back. They laid down flat in the truck bed out of view so not to draw heat from the cops. "Sky ever blue eh?" Chris said as Matt clumsily turned corners and eased through intersections. They held their cans of beer steadily on their chests and lifted their heads slightly to sip. Norman could feel the fall air getting colder, piercing his mid-afternoon buzz. He knew in a couple weeks his jean jacket wouldn't cut it and that he'd have to find something warmer soon.

A couple of other guys jumped in and laid beside them on the hard, treaded plastic liner while the chatter of more female voices could be heard piling into the front. Chris handed them beer and they were instant friends, albeit temporary ones. The slowly setting sun made the silhouettes on the sides of the buildings in their peripheral vision from the truck bed floor harsh again, and suddenly the truck was stopped and they were jumping over its side and stumbling down the stairs into Matt's apartment.

Matt put the music on loud. He was proud of the stereo system that he bought with his decent mine salary. The guitar lead of Oasis' "What's the Story Morning Glory" rattled the ear drums of the ten people crammed into his low basement apartment. The air was soon thick with choking cigarette smoke that didn't seem to bother anyone. "These guys are from England but they're fuckin' awesome!" shouted Matt. "Fuck these English queers!" shouted someone else in response. It was a random, nonsensical response that had the rest of them laughing.

Norman sat on the couch chatting with a young Ojibway woman whose name he already forgot. She was from a reserve near Marathon, though. That he remembered. She was short and voluptuous, with eyes wider than the typical young *Anishinaabekwe*. Her black hair was long and smooth. I wanna touch her hair, he kept thinking. As far as he was concerned, he was back on the market. Denise just dumped him that morning. He was on a sloppy prowl.

The rock songs blended into each other and the tables and kitchen counter began filling up with empty beer bottles and cans. "Alright, I'm gonna put on a fuckin' go song!" announced Matt. He stumbled into the living room and tripped on the carpet, crashing head first into the TV. The rest of them broke out in ugly, boozy, cackling. He collapsed giggling on the floor before getting up to fumble with the compact disc cases on top of the speaker. His blue t-shirt was soaked with sweat and spilled beer. He closed one eye to focus on the plastic Soundgarden Superunknown case and clumsily pulled it from the backing and slammed it into the tray of the CD player. "Fuckin' Spoonmaaaaan! He talks about Indians in this song!"

It was dark outside and the sharply frigid air snapped Norman to, momentarily. They were walking to a bar. He wasn't sure where, but looking around him he noticed their numbers had apparently dwindled slightly. A couple of them passed out back at the apartment, sure to get up later and keep partying. He could no longer see the woman he was hoping to eventually get in bed.

Once again, they found themselves in a bar with more loud music, more beer, and more thick cigarette smoke. They inhabited a large booth in the back corner. It was early in the evening and there were hardly any other people in the large, hall-style bar with a high ceiling and neon beer brand signs lining the walls. The waitress came with a round of beer and shots. And she came with more. The table, sticky and soaked with spilled beer, ashes and butts became a foul blend of the byproducts of vices.

Conversations were irrelevant and pointless. The priority was to get drunk. They did it as a collective to feel better about themselves, to honour the social contract. And, amid the ridiculous cacophony, Norman blacked out again, for the second night in a row.

His next memory was getting picked up off the sidewalk by one of the other nameless drunks in their entourage. He ran his hand across his face and looked at it to check for blood. Nothing. He must have just stumbled and fallen. "Where are we going?" he slurred. His temporary buddy said something about another party. Norman concentrated hard on putting one foot in front of the other. He didn't feel cold anymore. He looked around and only recognized Matt and three others from the start of the bender earlier that afternoon. He remembered that all the ladies who joined them were gone, and his chances at snagging as an officially single man were growing slim.

They stumbled up a fire escape and were soon meeting a handful of other boozers in a sparse, dingy apartment. Introductions were brief and sloppy, and cans of beer were immediately placed in hands. Everything and everyone looked the same to Norman. His head became heavy and he couldn't muster any energy to speak. He must have eventually said something, though, because he ended up on the floor after a sobering punch to the nose. A black then white flash exploded in his vision, and his blurry eyes struggled to focus on the growing red spot on the floor just centimetres from his face. He knew it was his blood. Before his vision had a chance to clear, someone was pulling him up by the armpits and they were soon outside again, carefully stepping down the black steel stairs.

There was another bar. There were more strangers. There were even more lapses in memory in between visions of glasses of beer, overturned tables, and smashed bottles. He heard songs he recognized, but never remembered the names. Then, there was what seemed to be a major blackout before he snapped to in the back of a car on the highway, holding a beer. "Isn't that right Normy?" he heard from the driver, who he saw taking a swig of a white can. He recognized the voice but couldn't put his finger on who it was. "Fuckin' eh bro, those assholes don't know shit!" was all he blurted out. The three others crammed in the back seat with him cackled. The cigarette smoke made his stomach turn and he felt along the upholstered side of the door for the window crank and opened it for some fresh air.

The car took a familiar left. It drove down a straight dirt road for a few minutes, headlights pointed straight into the darkness, not revealing anything but gravel ahead and bare trees on the sides. The driver eventually parked the car in front of a vast open darkness that Norman recognized as water. They all got out, and someone went to the back of the trunk to open another case of beer. Norman soon found another beer in his hand and opened it, and that was his last memory before he woke up on a couch to the sounds of the chatter of children.

Norman opened his eyes. He surveyed the room quickly before moving. His peripheral vision was blurry, so he couldn't make out any of the photos on the walls or on the shelves. Cartoons played on the TV to the left of the couch. A little boy and a little girl sat on the floor staring at the animated colours glowing from the screen. He looked out the wide picture window, and was able to orient himself with the familiar barren trees outside. The leaves had long fallen from them, and although they were a little taller than the last time he saw them, the white birch trees that dominated the forest outside were unmistakable. He used to stare at them when he was as young as the little kids on the floor. He was back in his childhood home. The home that now belonged to his brother Edgar.

Norman lifted his head and propped himself up on his right elbow. His head was stuck in the neutral hum of intoxication, keeping any sort of immediate pain or deeper self-awareness at bay. How the fuck did I get here, he thought. Before he could start digging through the vile piles of memories his mind could scrape together from the night before, Edgar suddenly appeared from down the hallway. Norman's heart started beating faster.

"Well well well," he declared. "Look who's up! Rise and shine, sweetheart!" Norman's heart eased a bit once he heard his older brother's somewhat cheery tone. Five-year-old Dylan and two-year-old Clara turned around from the TV. Their young eyes darted back and forth between their father and their uncle. "Nice to see you, little brother!" Edgar continued.

"Hey man," was all Norman replied.

"To what do we owe this gracious visit?"

"Your guess is as good as mine."

"Well, you made it here anyway. You musta been in autopilot by the end of it."

Norman was used to blacking out and not knowing how he ended up places. But it was always a little shocking at first to realize it.

"Get up," Edgar continued. "Let's have some breakfast." Norman's nose had taken another beating the night before, and the blood clots kept him from smelling the sizzling bacon coming from the kitchen. He looked behind Edgar to see Alana leaning over the stove. She turned around. "Oh hey Norm!" she said, almost happily. Norman knew he'd have an uncomfortable discussion with them eventually, but they never judged him—to his face, anyway—and at that moment he was feeling a bit better about being home.

"Come on kids," said Alana. "Breakfast's ready." The siblings ran to the table, where Edgar lifted Clara into her high chair and propped Dylan on his booster seat. Norman slowly upright, stood up, and made his way into the kitchen half of the main room of the house. Edgar went back to the stove where Alana dished out the eggs and bacon. From behind they looked similar—long ponytails running down the spines of wide backs. They just had different coloured t-shirts and Alana was nearly a head shorter than her husband. One by one, Edgar brought the plates to the table and they both sat down to start eating.

Norman had little appetite but ate anyway. He wasn't ready to talk, but he felt the need to know how he ended up back on Birchbark—more than an hour's drive from Sudbury. He picked up a piece of greasy bacon and shoved the whole thing in his mouth. It was chewy and salty.

"So how are things in Sudbury?" asked Alana from his right, starting conversation.

"They've been better," Norman admitted.

"You still staying at … uh …" she struggled to remember his now-ex's name.

"Denise's?"

"Yeah, Denise's."

"Nah, we broke up. Yesterday."

"Aw, sorry to hear that." She looked down into the yellow yolks of her fried eggs before piercing them with her fork.

"I think that's how I ended up on the bender that brought me here," he matter-of-factly admitted.

Dylan turned to Alana. "Mommy, what's a bender?" he asked.

"That's when you try to have too much fun but get sick," she half-joked. "See Uncle Norm? Does he look sick?"

"Really sick!" He giggled, his parents laughed, and Norman couldn't help but smirk.

Norman turned to Edgar, sitting across from him. "So I gotta come straight out and ask. How did I get here?"

"Well, I heard someone come in the front door around five this morning," Edgar said. "I grabbed my baseball bat and came out of the room. I turned on the light here and saw you rummaging around the kitchen. You're lucky I turned the light on or I woulda been swinging away!"

"I don't think your eyes coulda gotten much blacker," joked Alana.

"Jesus Chr-" Norman started, before catching himself.

"We talked for about a minute before you passed out," Edgar continued. "You were pretty gooned, man."

Norman just shook his head.

"You said you saw Brian Whitesky at the bar in Sudbury. They drove in just for the night to party, and that you hitched a ride back here with them. I guess you guys were drinking down by the beach before your autopilot kicked in and brought you back here."

"Autopilot saves my ass again," this time he didn't hold up from swearing in front of the kids. It didn't register with them anyway.

"You started talking about some other stuff before passing out on the couch. I tried to get you up to go to Stan's room but you wouldn't move."

Norman took quick bites during Edgar's recap and was close to finishing his breakfast. The eggs tasted bland and their mushy texture in his mouth made his stomach turn slightly. Alana noticed the unsettled look on his face.

"I think you need a bit more rest, bud," she said as she slapped his right thigh and squeezed it. "When you're done eating you can go lay down in Stan's room."

"Alright, thanks," he said. He finished eating silently, while Edgar turned to his son. "So you wanna go outside later and shoot the puck around, big guy?" Dylan smiled widely and nodded affirmatively. He was old enough for house league hockey now, but Edgar wanted to make sure he got the feel of a stick and skates before signing him up. He and Alana decided to wait until next season.

In the middle of the hockey talk, Norman stood up to go to the room. Edgar looked up at him. "We gotta go into town to do some shopping," he said. "We might not be here when you get up. But you know where everything is."

"Alright, thanks bro," he said. He took a few easy steps down the hall, turned left into his little brothers room, and collapsed face first onto the bed. He fell asleep almost immediately. Alana walked over to the room to close the door and give her brother-in-law a bit of privacy in order to hopefully re-instill a shred of dignity.

The incessant light and chemical smell of the waiting room made him sick to his stomach. Norman stood with his back against the wall, his legs nearly crippled by grief. He stared down at his feet. His undone white running shoes were stained brown and grey. The laces were tied in knots at the end, making them easy to slip on and off. He watched as the tears from his own eyes fell on and around his feet. He had never felt emotional devastation like this before and he knew it would haunt him for the rest of his life. He wasn't sure how he'd get over it, and he already wanted to forget it.

There was a lot of space between him and his siblings. To him, they felt more distant than ever. He wanted this tragedy to bring them closer together, but he felt the sorrow prying them apart like a lever between two stubborn boards in a crumbling wall. Just then Edgar grabbed him by the shoulder and pulled him in tight for a comforting embrace. Norman's shoulders and chest heaved as he sobbed into his brother's jacket collar. Otherwise the waiting room was eerily silent, save for the buzzing of the unnatural lights overhead.

With his eyes closed tightly in the safe confines of his brother's arms, he thought of his sister Eva and how much she meant to him. He remembered her smile. She was both strong and gentle, embodying a genuine kindness rarely seen in the world. She was his younger sister, but he looked up to her drive and her determination. He knew she was going to amount to something big. She already made them all so incredibly proud. No one could ever replace her and the thought of this made him sob harder.

Norman heard his baby sister Maria sobbing too. This was especially crushing. He rubbed Edgar's back with his hands and moved slowly away from them. "Thank you, brother," he said. "We'll get through this," he said. Norman turned to look for Maria in order to go to her and comfort her. She was sitting on one of the hard chairs on the other side of the room. The slender, long-haired figure who had her arms wrapped around Maria to console her was Eva.

Norman sat on the side of Stanley's bed, now close to being sober and deeply ashamed. The tragedies in his life had started to blur together in his memory. He looked up at the walls in Stanley's room to try to distract himself. A large poster hung over his desk, commemorating the Toronto Blue Jays' 1992 World Series win. Stanley put that up when he came home for Christmas break that year. Norman remembered watching it on TV at a bar somewhere. He couldn't remember where, but the last out in extra innings was unforgettable. Memories of Stanley morphed into memories of Eva, since they both had left for school. Memories of Eva quickly became reflections on tragedy, and that scene in the hospital waiting room once again paralleled the loss of his parents. For a sober mind in these familiar surroundings, it was impossible to keep those solemn thoughts and memories suppressed. He needed a drink.

Norman didn't bother looking anywhere in the house because he knew he wouldn't find any booze. There was an eerie silence hanging in the house. That meant the family was in town. As mental and emotional clarity returned, the despair of the Gibsons' losses came oozing through the cracks in the walls he created to block the unresolved grief. If he were anywhere but here, he could handle it. But with pictures and relics of the dead surrounding him, he had to get out. He stood up and bolted out of the room. He grabbed his jacket by the front entrance and flung the door open. Staring straight ahead, he jumped down the stairs and strode steadily to the main road, and turned left.

The cold, overcast sky was like a harsh weave of stinging thorns on his hardened face. The wind picked up from the west, pelting him with cold rain and small pellets of hail. He ignored them, focusing only on the tempestuous vast blue water directly ahead of him. He walked steadfast and determined, trying to chase everything that was pecking at his mind and spirit like vultures dining on a deer's carcass in the thick of the bush.

A thin layer of wet sand coated the beach. Norman stepped through it, kicking up the darker sand and leaving lighter footprints of the dry beach beneath. He stopped a metre from the heaving shoreline. The white-capping waves churned heavily towards him. The wind howled and nudged him to his left. His fists clenched and he remembered everything. How his family fell apart after his parents died. How he ran from the pain of his sister's killing. How he desired vengeance on the head of the white man whose name he couldn't remember.

And in an impulsive lapse of despair, Norman walked into the water. He waded in up to his knees. The frigid lake bit sharply into his feet and calves like dozens of large, black leeches ready to suck the life out of him. He gritted his teeth tightly together as the breath in his chest accelerated out of control. He walked in further still, up to his waist. His testicles retreated upwards and he gasped harshly as his hands breached the surface. He loosened his fingers as if to offer them up to the hungry water. They were icy and numb instantly.

The sorrow and the rage wrestled within him, and the grey horizon above the blue turbulence in his eyesight became a bright red flash. The image pulsed before him with each heartbeat. He walked forward, up to his neck, blinded by his floundering spirit in the throes of despair. The pounding in his ears deafened him, flooding out the shouts coming from behind.

To make it all stop, he submerged his head and the red became black. He was at peace, and he relaxed. He was ready to welcome death, when a pair of strong arms suddenly yanked him back to the surface.

EDGAR
Summer 1997

Edgar sat in the near-scorching humid heat of the dark sweat-lodge with his legs crossed on the cedar bows. His back rested against the frame of saplings as sweat dripped from every pore of his skin. The ceremony was silent for a moment, in between songs and speakers. With his eyes wide open, he wiped the sweat from his forehead with the back of his hand to keep it from stinging. He surveyed the inside of the lodge as he always did, not able to see anything but scanning for any signs of life through the darkness. Often when he did this, he could make out the skeletal frame of young trees that held up the tarp. When the heat became too much to bear, he would lean over to breathe from the comforting confines of the cedar. He would visualize the compact green leaves outlined in orange and fully illuminating in a blast of healing through the darkness. These were his personal visions for this process. It was a ceremony he held in extremely high regard since it came into his life just eight years before.

Across the lodge by the eastern doorway, the water drum sounded. It beat slowly four times, before starting into the steady rhythm of a song. Sitting by the flap that covered the doorway, elder Jim Daniels began singing an honour song. He came up from Manitoulin Island just for the night to conduct the sweatlodge. Edgar and the eleven other men and women joined in. The thick black air seemed to amplify their voices and the beat by impeding their vision. To Edgar, it felt like a transcendental elevation of his spirit into the low ceiling of the structure, followed by a brief descent of his spirit's vessel under the cedar branches into the ground below him.

The song ended, and it was Norman's turn to speak. He sat to Edgar's left, with their aunt Kathy and Jared Wilson, Stanley's friend, between them. The darkness made for a gaping silence, albeit brief. Norman cleared his throat and started talking.

"*Boozhoo,*" he said loudly.

"*Boozhoo,*" the rest responded.

"*Norman n'dizhnikaaz. Giigoo n'dodem. Wiigwaasitiging n'doonjiba,*"

"*Hooooo,*" his friends and relatives responded in unison,

acknowledging his introduction in the Ojibway language. It was a proud moment for Norman—and especially for his aunt and his brother in the sweat—to be able to lead with the most basic of opening statements in his native tongue. They all shared in that pride of knowing just a bit of the old language.

Jim was able to confirm what they had speculated all along—that the Gibsons were in fact from the Fish Clan. By tracing their lineage to other relatives on his own reserve, he found a common great-grandfather who passed that knowledge down. In the Anishinaabe clan system, that identity is carried patriarchally from generation to generation. But for a variety of repressive reasons, that information never made it to their father, Bill Gibson. If it did, he chose to ignore it because of the shame attached to the "old ways" when he was growing up. Reclaiming that knowledge and passing it on in the old language was a huge victory for his children.

Norman continued. "I want to say *chi-miigwech* to everyone for coming here tonight. To our uncle here who travelled a great distance to bring us this beautiful healing ceremony. I want to say *chi-miigwech* for this gift of the sweatlodge. To the grandfathers. To the Little Boy water drum. To all of you for sharing with us tonight."

Edgar listened intently and calmly. It was comforting hearing his little brother speak here. The first few times he brought him into a sweat it was much more intense. Norman had a lot of healing to do. But now, he was on his way.

"I sit here, humble and thankful," Norman said. "I was living in a very bad way before getting on this path. I was dealing with a lot of pain. But I didn't know it at the time. I guess I was keeping the pain away with drugs and alcohol. I was a drunk for a really long time. I didn't have no work. I didn't treat people with respect. I didn't love myself."

Edgar leaned forward to put his face into the cedar.

"I lost my parents when I was just nineteen. It was devastating. I stayed sad for a long time after that. I guess I never really got over it. But I didn't talk about it with no one. I couldn't live in their house no more because everything reminded me of them. So I just took off. I left my brothers and my little sister behind."

Edgar had heard Norman recount his struggles in sweats past. It was hard for him to listen to his little brother slowly pull himself out of his emotional ditch at first, but as Norman slowly got to his feet, Edgar actually enjoyed hearing him share his story. To him, it proved his brother's resolve to get better and to live in a more positive way. *Mino bmaadziwin* is what they called it in their language—"the good life".

"I went to the city just to get away," Norman went on. "I drank a lot at first to try to get over it. And I eventually did. It wasn't a good way to deal with it though. I thought I was better. But then my little sister was killed in Toronto."

To his right, Kathy shuddered.

"All that grief came back," Norman spoke slowly. "I didn't really deal with it in the first place. I just chased it away for a while with booze. And when it came back it was worse. It came back with a lot of anger. I was a really angry man. I still am. But I'm working on dealing with that. That's why I'm here."

"*Hooooo*," the sweaters responded, and Jim beat the drum four times quickly.

"I was filled with enough rage to kill a man. I wanted to find the guy who killed my sister and make him pay. I used to picture what I'd do to him. I thought about it almost every day. It was a sick way to live. When I didn't wanna think about it no more, I went to the liquor store or to the bar. When I worked I could keep my mind off it. But when I was alone I had to drink.

"Eventually that lifestyle wore me down. Four years of my life just blurred together. I couldn't even tell you what happened in that time. I have no good memories from then. I decided at some point that I was gonna die. If the booze didn't take me out, someone else would. I didn't have no real friends. You make a lot of enemies in that way of life. And if nothing else took me out, I decided I'd do it myself."

Edgar remembered that cold November day almost two years earlier. Norman showed up out of the blue in the middle of the night, wasted. As he slept it off the next day, Edgar, Alana and the kids went into Waverley to pick up some groceries. He remembered expecting Norman to be there for at least a couple of weeks. When they got back home late in the afternoon, Norman was nowhere to be found. They left him sleeping in Stanley's old room. Something called Edgar to the water, and he got back in their minivan and drove less than a minute to the beach. He saw a dark figure wading out in the water. He knew it was Norman. He jumped out of the van and sprinted to the shore, shouting his brother's name. He reached him just as his head went under.

"All that came to a really dark moment," Norman continued. "And I'm not really ready to talk about that yet." He cleared his throat again.

"But I wanna say *chi-miigwech* to my brother here, and my auntie, for showing me this sweatlodge and this beautiful way of life."

"*Hooooo*," the group acknowledged.

"It really has saved my life," Norman's voice cracked. He got it back together quickly. "I know I wouldn't be here without it. And I wanna say *chi-miigwech* to all my relatives and friends in here, and to our uncle Jim. Thank you for listening to me and for supporting me. I still got a lot of work to do. But I know I can do it with your help. *Miigwech*."

"*Hooo-waaa!*"

Jim beat the drum again and offered a traveling song. With that, the sweat concluded, and the firekeeper outside opened the flap to the eastern doorway. A sharp orange glow flooded the black view, and softened as eyes adjusted to the still raging fire just a few metres from the sweatlodge. Edgar looked around to see the soothing light of the fire splash across the different shades of brown skin circled around the pit of still-glowing stones.

The evening summer air was hot, but it was cool relief as it entered the lodge and danced with the steamy atmosphere inside. The moist air billowed out of the flap, as the people inside gathered their towels and got up on their hands and knees to crawl out of the short structure. Each touched the cooling, cracked stones that were once so intensely hot they glowed orange and said "Miigwech". As they reached the flap, the fire-keeper Danny Whitesky held out his hand and helped them to their feet.

"Did Uncle Jim make ya burn?" he asked Edgar as he pulled him up.

"Every time!" he responded. Danny chuckled. Once they were all out, they stood around the fire and towelled off. Kathy turned to Norman and held her arms open wide for a hug. She smiled, and he obliged. They held each other tightly for a good few seconds. She wore a full bathing suit under a pair of shorts, and the top was soaked through. So were Norman's long gym shorts. Under other circumstances it would have been an uncomfortable embrace, but it didn't matter in this post-sweat comedown. Edgar waited for them to break before taking his turn hugging his brother and his aunt. They didn't say a word.

They usually held their sweats in the yard behind Kathy's house near the school. She and Harvey had a lot of room, both in the back for the ceremony and in the driveway for cars to park, so she was only too happy to host. Edgar and Norman said their farewells to everyone who came, and thanked Jim again for coming up. It was about 10PM, so he had enough time to drive back to the island before it was too late. He also had his niece Nicole with him, with whom Edgar had done some youth outreach work: cultural teachings and workshops to reign young people into positive living. Edgar walked to the family minivan with Norman close behind. They got in and Edgar turned the key in the ignition.

"Good one tonight eh?" he mentioned to Norman.

"Yeah," he said. "I'm starting to really get used to the heat."

"Oooooh tough guy. We're gonna have to start cranking it up then!"

"*Pfffft*, bring it on then!"

"As if," he smiled. "You'll be tugging at the flap, crying to Uncle Jim to let you out!"

"Not even!"

Edgar backed up and drove out on to the dirt road. Home was just a few short minutes away in the south end of the community. He and his brother sat in silence for the quick jaunt. But Edgar's heart was full of love and pride. He greatly enjoyed these moments with his little brother and his aunt, and with anyone else from their family and their community, really. It was a path he decided to follow long ago, and gradually, those close to him were joining.

They drove with the windows open through the dark July night. Frogs bleated from the swamp behind the baseball field. The headlights highlighted the backs of three teenaged boys walking with traffic on the side of the road. Under the beaks of their backwards caps were large backpacks, filled with what both Edgar and Norman assumed was beer. They each kept their thoughts to themselves, not to ignore the usual habits of rez youth, but simply because they each knew the other noticed. Shortly after they passed the boys, they heard loud music blaring from one of the driveways to the right. The steady beat and bass hinted at rap. Norman tried to see where it was coming from, but the thick leaves on the trees obscured his view. Party's probably at the Taylors' place, he thought, and again kept his judgment to himself by saying nothing.

The lights were on when they pulled up to the Gibson house. The brothers stepped out of the van, and Edgar led the way up the stairs. He opened the door and walked in to see Alana lying on the couch, watching a movie. Julia Roberts was on the screen. She looked in their direction.

"Hey," she said. "How was it?"

"*Aapchi gzhiso*," Edgar replied. "It was really hot!"

"Oh yeah? How'd you do Normy?"

"No problem," he said with a smirk.

"Are the kids in bed?" Edgar asked.

"Yeah, they wanted to wait up for you guys but I think all that swimming today did them in."

"Yep, they're Gibsons then," Norman affirmed. He turned to walk down to the basement. He had taken over Maria's old living space after she got a full-time job in the Soo. He was now a thirty-year-old man, so Edgar and Alana wanted to give him as much personal space and privacy as possible. He arranged the whole downstairs area into his own quasi-bachelor pad. He wasn't working on anything steady yet, but his brother and sister-in-law thought it was important to give him a good opportunity to clean up and get his life back on track. He was also great with his niece and nephew, and could be counted on for childcare almost anytime.

Upstairs, Edgar walked over to the couch to kiss his wife. He sat down in the armchair across from her. "Yep, you were definitely sweating tonight," she said. He was emanating heat and his virile scent and demeanour carried across the room. Alana smiled and peaked at him out of the corner of her eye as he monitored the TV screen.

"Which one's this?" he asked.

"Honestly I dunno," she replied. "I was just flipping around. The ball game finished just before you guys got in."

"Did they win?"

"Yeah, Clemens was pitching. That's pretty much a given whenever he's on the mound. Good thing he was though. Their bats were pretty weak tonight."

"I still can't believe they got him."

"Yeah really."

Creating a comfortable life together was easy and natural for Edgar and Alana. They met in the beer tent at a ball tournament in Sudbury when they were twenty-one and twenty, respectively. Edgar was playing for the Birchbark men, and she was playing for the Stoney Inlet women. Edgar was drawn to her smile and athletic build. She was drawn to his stoic, strong appearance. They hit it off immediately, and were bound by their love of sports and their desire to work with Native youth. They crossed paths again at a training course months later in the Soo, and the rest was history.

Alana pulled herself up to sit straight on the couch. "So..." she said. "Do you think Norm's gonna be crashed soon?"

"Oh yeah, that was a scorcher," Edgar replied. "I could tell he was feeling it. He's probably already asleep."

It quickly dawned on him what she was getting at. "So why do you ask, hmmmm?" he queried with a wink.

"No reason," she smirked, then bit her bottom lip and lowered her eyelids. She glanced coyly back at the TV as if to briefly ignore him. He tilted his head down and raised an eyebrow.

Alana picked up the remote control and turned off the TV. She stood up and walked towards Edgar sitting on the chair on her way down the hall. She let her fingers run up his bare forearm as she went by. The quick contact sparked a fire deep in Edgar. He got up and followed her to stoke the flames and build them even higher.

He was sprawled out on the couch in his apartment in Birchbark's six-unit housing complex when he got the phone call. Edgar had been living in the building community members commonly called the "Sixplex" for about eight months. After dropping out of university, he moved back into his parents' house for about a month, but the shame of failing in the city motivated him to get his own place to be an "adult". There was a vacancy in the Sixplex and Kathy fast-tracked him through the housing list to get him in there. The only stipulation was he had to work as well, as per the band-housing bylaw. She got him a maintenance job at the water treatment plant too.

The independence appealed to him. Also, he could drink alcohol here on his own without feeling guilty, away from the disappointed scrutiny of his parents and the judging gazes of his aunts and uncles. The frustrating hypocrisy for Edgar was that most of them drank too. But he tried to ignore that frustration, and the booze helped with that. It was Saturday night, and he was badly hungover from partying in Waverley with some of the King boys the night before. Another beer helped with that too.

The rabbit ears on his TV only picked up three stations out of Sudbury. He had it locked on the one that broadcast a popular late night comedy and variety show. The cold beer slowly brought back a familiar dulling buzz, but Edgar told himself that was to get his mind back in order and not to get drunk again. He purposely ignored invitations to party on the rez that night because he was determined to cut down on his boozing.

He let the phone ring into silence more than a few times earlier in the evening, knowing that picking up would have led him back down into the sloppy pit of vice.

Shortly after 11PM, the phone rang again. It went on and on, and Edgar stayed put on the couch, staring at the TV and trying to tune out the bizarre vibrato coming from the small, simple black phone mounted on the wall by the fridge. He counted fifteen rings before it stopped. Figured it was Bruce calling from wherever people were partying on the rez tonight. The thought of the rest of his friends being wasted and trying to coax him out annoyed him. He wondered why people around him felt the need to drag others along when they drank. He figured it was just because misery loves company, as the old saying goes.

Less than a minute later the phone started to ring again. "For fuck's sake!" Edgar said aloud. He knew the calls would likely keep up if he didn't just pick up and insist that he wasn't coming out tonight. If the message didn't stick, he'd just leave the phone off the hook so he could get some sleep. By the seventh ring, he knew it wouldn't stop, so he stood up and walked over to the wall to pick it up.

He blurted out an annoyed, "Hey, who is this?"

"Is this Edgar Gibson?" the voice on the other end of the line asked.

"Yeah. Who's calling?"

"My name is Constable McLeod with the Espanola Detachment of the Ontario Provincial Police," the man said. "I'm sorry to call you this late."

"What's going on?"

"I'm afraid I have some bad news. You better sit down."

Edgar's head spun and his chest felt like it caved in. His stomach jumped and he wanted to puke. He braced himself for news of death.

The morning after the sweat, Edgar was on the road east to Sudbury to visit with a group of Anishinaabe inmates at the Ramsey Detention Centre. The maximum security facility housed boys who committed a wide range of serious crimes from aggravated assault to auto theft to murder. As young offenders, their sentences stretched from just a couple of weeks to four years. Most of them were Ojibway kids from reserves in the area, all the way up to northwestern Ontario. And that's where Edgar came in, a youth worker with a considerable knowledge of the culture.

Edgar officially started working as Birchbark's community youth worker the spring before Stanley left for University. He had just passed his six-year anniversary in the position. With only a semester of post-secondary education under his belt, he wasn't really qualified for the job. But he was overqualified compared to the rest of the applicants at the time; many of whom had barely finished high school. Plus, he had held summer positions and done a lot of volunteer work in similar capacities many times since coming back to the rez. That choppy resumé wouldn't fly in most non-Native communities, but Birchbark desperately needed a young person they could pin the "role model" tag on and provide just a shred of guidance to the young people. By the time he got the job, Edgar was sober, and following the traditional ways. He was twenty-five then, still learning a lot about himself not only as a young man, but as an Anishinaabe. Now at thirty-one, he was proud, confident, and happy.

Short evergreen trees sprouted from the rocky terrain that lined each side of Highway 17. They were like promising hints of life in an otherwise bleak and barren landscape. That's what Edgar looked for in the young people he worked with. For many of them, the culture had been clear-cut from their minds and their spirits. And that was done generations before them. They didn't understand the pain, confusion and anger they carried. Those powerful emotions filled the void in the identity that was passed down to them by their parents and their grandparents.

But in the desolate lands of their spirits, Edgar could see the budding saplings. He wanted to nurture those tiny traces of goodness. Some called him naive. Others told him to give up. But he dedicated himself to fostering hope in those young people, one at a time. Once in a while they took to him and his support almost immediately. For most of them, though, it took months of regular visits and activities to get them on a path to healing. A few would reject his help, only to return to him as young adults. A few would give up altogether and kill themselves. No matter how many sweats or fasts he did himself or for them, Edgar could never really get over those ones.

He looked in the rearview mirror and noticed a transport truck coming up quickly behind him. This was the Trans-Canada Highway, after all, so there was always a lot of traffic like this. He caught a glimpse of his own eyes before turning them back to the road in front of him. They were narrow, underneath thick eyebrows. Crow's feet had started to sprout from the corners. That didn't bother him, though, because he was never vain. He rubbed his wide nose with the back of his right hand and scratched the dark brown skin stretched across his high cheekbone. The short sleeves on his button-up blue shirt were tight on his arms, so he pulled them down. He reached for the paper coffee cup in the holder beneath the radio console and lifted the plastic lid to his wide mouth.

The bright summer sun was high in the sheer blue sky by the time he pulled into Sudbury. He visited the Ramsey Centre at least a dozen times in the past, so finding it through the city streets had become second nature. He bypassed the downtown core, and in about fifteen minutes he had found his way on to the industrial road that concealed the youth prison from the rest of the community. From a distance, the front of the building looked like a small elementary school with its grey bricks and green metal roof. Up closer, the high fences could be seen towering from behind, and the small, dark windows of thick glass suggested less a place of learning but rather one of remorse and punishment.

Edgar parked the van and walked around to the lift gate at the back to grab his medicine bundle and his hand drum. In his black cotton bag were small pouches containing the essential medicines—tobacco, sage, sweetgrass, and cedar—along with an abalone shell, his eagle feather, and a shaker made of hardened deerhide with a fish painted on it. His hand drum was in a separate blue and black cloth bag. He picked up the satchels and held them close to his body under his left arm while he shut and locked the gate with his other arm.

He walked up to the heavily fortified steel front door and hit the intercom button to the right. They expected him, but he had to announce himself anyway. Once buzzed in, he had to sign in and then subject himself to a rigorous security screening. That meant opening his bundle and placing all the sacred items out onto a table for inspection. Edgar found this process disrespectful and a little invasive at first, but he got used to it and focused on what needed to be accomplished. Just having those medicines inside a youth detention centre was a small triumph for the culture itself.

Getting to the point of infusing Anishinaabe customs into corrections was a long journey. In the legal aftermath of Eva's killing, Edgar befriended one of the Crown Prosecutors involved with the case—a man named Lorne Friedman. Edgar had a difficult time trusting or believing anyone attached to that process when it got underway eight years earlier. But Friedman, a short, stalky man with short, curly salt-and-pepper hair, took Edgar and Kathy under his wing from the beginning. He was tough, but kind; honest and straightforward and consoled them when they needed it. Despite the crushing outcome, with Lorne, the family had a new friend for life.

Little did they know that Lorne was a key figure in many justice circles. He was a veteran of the provincial legal scene, and as one of the most respected lawyers in Ontario, he had a lot of pull. When Edgar told him he had started a new career as a youth worker, Lorne rallied the corrections authorities to consider a new approach in counselling young Aboriginal inmates in the system. The Ramsey Centre reluctantly agreed to have him come in on a trial basis. That was a year and a half earlier. The response from the young Ojibway inmates was so great, the visits became almost monthly, and Edgar soon hoped to be there weekly.

Edgar also had an ally on the inside. One of his old classmates at Waverley High School, Steve Dubois, was a teacher at Ramsey. He also went to university in Ottawa when Edgar did. But Steve stuck it out. As Edgar put the medicines and his drum back in their bags, he noticed Steve approaching out of the corner of his eye.

"Eddie!" he yelled mildly. "How the hell are ya?"

Edgar turned to shake his hand. "Pretty good thanks, buddy!" They gripped hands firmly and shook twice. "How's your summer been?"

"Ah, not bad," his old friend said. He was tall and slender, in a white polo shirt and khaki pants. His face was warm with a wide smile. A two-way radio was clipped to his belt, along with a couple of other nondescript small, black canvas pouches. "I'm going on holidays in a couple weeks."

"Oh yeah? Going anywhere?"

"Just heading to the lake with the family. The kids got the swimming bug now, so there's no keeping them from the water."

"Oh man, I hear ya." Steve's two daughters were roughly the same age as Edgar's kids.

Edgar changed direction. "So how's the group these days?" It had been nearly a month and a half since his last visit.

"Let's just say they're getting a little restless. The nice weather isn't helping."

"Hmmmm."

"A couple of them really beat up Christian last week. It was pretty rough."

"How's he doing now?"

"Better, but he really doesn't fit in with any of them. I think he's too young to really relate to any of them."

"I think trying hard to fit in is what got him here in the first place."

"Yeah, no doubt."

"Well, are they all ready?"

"They should be. They're doing some math homework now, but I'm sure they would love the interruption. I'll take you down there."

"Okay, cool."

Steve turned and walked down the hall, and Edgar followed. On the inside, it actually looked like a regular school. The walls were made of coated cinder blocks painted white, and save for the heavily reinforced windows and doors, the classrooms actually resembled a typical high school. It surprised Edgar at first, but now he was used to it.

At the end of the hall they stopped in front of a door with a dream catcher on it. It was their usual math class, but it was the only room the provincial corrections authorities let them smudge in. As such, it needed some sort of "traditional" decoration to mark it. The guard monitoring the six boys inside saw them approach through the window, and got up to let Edgar in.

"Come by my office before you go," said Steve. "I have something for you."

Edgar nodded and walked into the classroom. He immediately bellowed "*Aanii*, boys!" to jovially break the institutional ice. No matter which reserves these kids were from, he knew they needed a dose of the Anishinaabe free spirit and humour.

"*Aaaaniiiiiii!*" they deeply voiced back in unison. The six boys with shaved heads and orange sweatshirts and sweatpants stood up from their desks. Their black velcro shoes shuffled around the tiled floor as they rearranged their chairs into a circle. Edgar peered into the bustling group to pinpoint Christian. The short, skinny fourteen-year-old with red acne speckling his brown face still had a black eye, but he was smiling. It was the kind of innocence Edgar saw in each of these boys that gave him hope they could turn things back around.

They organized themselves in red plastic classroom chairs in a circle fairly quickly, and Edgar joined them. He took the empty seat to Christian's right. He scanned the circle, which was down to six from eight the last time he visited them. That could be for a number of good or bad reasons: release, transfer, or violence. Edgar didn't dwell on that though, and was thankful for the time with the ones who had assembled here. There were no new faces.

"Good to see you guys today," he said once chairs settled.

"Good to see you too, bro," said Jacob, to his right. At seventeen, he was the eldest of the group and came from a reserve near Orillia. His hardened eyes spoke of tough teenage years, but there was a soft wisdom about them as well. If his eyes couldn't cut through a spirit, his broad shoulders and massive arms could make easy work of a body. He was the only one who truly intimidated Edgar, but he was also the friendliest. Jacob was in for severely beating another kid at school and putting him in a coma. The last Edgar heard, the victim had brain damage and would likely never fully recover.

"Miigwech for coming," Edgar heard Christian utter softly to his left. The rest of the group was rounded out clockwise to Christian's left by sixteen-year-old Dakota from near Kenora, fifteen-year-old Lance from near the Soo, sixteen-year-old James from Barrie, and fifteen-year-old Cody from outside of Sudbury.

Edgar turned to Christian. "Chris, do you want to start the smudge?" he asked. Christian's face lit up the last time he asked him, and Edgar knew the honour would be just as great for him this time. He got up quickly to get the ceremonial blanket that was folded up in a corner of the room. It was an exciting new realm for the young teen. Ironically, being in the confines of these thick, armoured walls with nowhere to go opened his eyes to the elaborate possibilities in the world outside. This exposure to traditional ceremony helped him step further away from his recent life of stealing cars and setting fires.

Christian returned to the circle and laid out the small, rectangular wool blanket on the floor. A bald eagle with its wings spread wide sprawled across the fabric, roughly the size of a common coffee table. Edgar handed him the medicine bundle and he knelt in front of the blanket. He carefully pulled out the shiny abalone shell, followed by the protected eagle feather and the bundle of sage. He unwrapped the sage and broke off a small handful, placing it into the shell. He opened the birchbark fold that encased the eagle feather and laid it beside the shell.

Edgar pulled a book of matches from his jeans pocket and handed it to him. Christian snapped one from the first row, folded the book backwards onto the match head, squeezed it against the ignition strip, and pulled the stick out swiftly. It sparked into an intense tiny explosion and settled as a flame. He brought it down to the sacred sage to light it on fire. The dried plant ignited quickly, and almost as quickly, Christian blew it out. He picked up the feather and fanned the smoulder- ing medicine in the shell, letting the aroma of the thick, potent, smoke build.

Soon, a reassuring layer of smudge floated in the air through- out the room. Christian took the shell in his left hand and the feather in his right, and went around the circle to smudge his counterparts. He fanned the burning sage and held it close to Dakota's chest. Dakota leaned over and ran his hands through the climbing smoke, before fanning it towards him. The scars on his scalp were easily visible to Christian through his buzz-cut hair. His long fingers with short nails cupped tightly together as he motioned a cleansing about his torso and his legs. Once finished, Dakota looked up at Christian with his blue eyes and said *Miigwech*.

The next three boys followed in a similar ritual until they were cleansed too. Then Christian came to Jacob. Edgar noticed a slight apprehension in his small steps as he approached the eldest boy in the group. Jacob's eyes were fixed harshly on Christian's, causing the younger of the two to look down at the smudge shell nervously. Jacob's intimidating gaze stayed on Christian's lowered brown eyelids as he fanned the sage smoke onto himself. He put his hands down on his lap and didn't say anything. The tension and intimidation were obvious to Edgar, and he made sure to smile at Christian as he came closer.

Christian fanned the burning sage in the shell a few more times. Edgar looked up into his eyes and saw the traces of fear and unease. He took his time while he smudged in an attempt to make the boy comfortable again in this proud new role. It was clear to him that if Jacob wasn't the one who beat Christian, he was the one who organized it. Edgar cupped both of his hands over the bowl and brought them to his mouth and nose. He harnessed the smudge smoke once again and ran his hands over his hair. He finished smudging and looked into the boys eyes, enunciating a resounding *Miigwech*.

The boy set the bowl and the feather back down on the blanket and took his seat to the left of Edgar. He shifted slightly and stared down at the medicines laid out on the floor. Beside him, Edgar reached down for his hand drum and drumstick. He held the drum in his left hand and ran his hand across the tight, yellow deer hide surface, as if to caress and massage it into song. He cleared his throat harshly and began to speak, introducing himself in Ojibway before welcoming the boys to the circle.

"I want to say *Miigwech* to each of you for joining me here in this circle today," he said. "It really lifts my spirit to see you guys so interested and enthusiastic in these traditions. And I know it's not just because you're getting out of math homework."

The group chuckled lightly together. Half of them leaned over with their elbows on their knees. The other half leaned back with their legs sticking straight out into the middle of the circle and their elbows crossed. "I'm gonna start off with a song," Edgar followed up. "This one is called the Bear Song. I know a couple of you must be Bear Clan. We talked last time about the clan system and what that means in Anishinaabe culture. The words in this song honour the spirit of that bear."

Edgar struck the drum four times before picking it up in a steady beat. After a few simple bars in 4/4 time, he closed his eyes and started to sing. None of the boys was brave enough to sing along, but Dakota and Christian both mouthed the words along with him. After four verses and four choruses, Edgar let out a mild "*hoowaa!*" and set the drum down gently on the blanket with the stick beside it.

He stared down at all the gifts laid out in front of him and was silent for a moment. He sat up straight and looked at each of the boys. Each bent their eyebrows down to give an illusion of toughness and mild ire. It was a front, Edgar knew, and he wondered if their eyes were stuck this way. It was his job to ease that hardened façade and give them the tools to remould it. He started talking. "So how you guys doing? Who wants to start?"

Dakota piped up "I'm going home in a month!" The excitement in his voice and his face revealed some of that innate innocence. The statement drew both smiles and scowls from his peers. Deep down, though, each was happy for him.

"Oh yeah, what you gonna do?" asked Edgar.

"I'm gonna go fishing at Lake of the Woods! Maybe see if I can go to some powwows too."

"Oh yeah, fishing's good up there eh? Ever caught a muskey?"

"Nah, but my cousin did once. My grandma has a big picture of him with it in a frame at her house."

"That's pretty cool. Well you better catch one this summer then!"

It was always necessary to break the ice this way, Edgar felt. After they all had a chance to warm up, he'd share a bit of traditional knowledge with them. He explained that he was from the Fish Clan and what that meant. He picked up from where he left off last time with clan knowledge—how each person and their families were part of a clan. The Bear Clan, for example, were the protectors of the community. The clan identity was passed down through the father. None of the boys knew which clan they belonged to, but he urged them to ask their uncles and grandparents when they got back home. Sadly, many of them didn't live with their parents, let alone have living ones. Tragedy appeared early in their lives and lingered, leading them down a path of destruction and despair.

Over the next hour, Edgar shared Nanabush stories, the often humorous and enlightening tales based on original man and his adventures through a blossoming new world. The stories made the boys laugh. Even if they'd heard some of the same ones from last time, they still enjoyed them because they became familiar and something they could be proud of and share.

"Once the crow was the most beautiful bird in creation," Edgar began. "But he was very vain and boastful." He went on to explain how one day Nanabush got so fed up with the crow that he decided to teach him a lesson in humility. He shoved the bird into the cold coals of a fire and split his tongue. "Now, the only sound you hear from a crow is 'caw'. Does that sound like anything to you guys?"

Jacob piped up. "Like the word for 'no' in Ojibway?"

"Yep, that's exactly it. The crow is forever remorseful for being vain. That's all it can say. My auntie told me that story when I was about your age."

It took them a while, but they asked questions and shared parts of their stories too. Edgar concluded the visit with an honour song on the hand drum. He wasn't sure when he'd be back to visit them, so he wanted to wish them safe travels if they got out before he got back.

Once the song was over, he walked around the circle to lead the round of handshakes. He started with Christian, who followed him. Edgar sat back down once he was finished with Jacob, and watched cautiously as Christian approached him. They shared a cordial, friendly handshake and Jacob even smiled at him. Edgar hoped this chipped away at whatever animosity the older boy held towards the younger one.

Edgar gathered his bundle and his drum, said *miigwech*, and the guard let him out into the hall. Another guard stood watching in the hallway, and directed him to Steve's office. Edgar nodded and turned the corner to see an open door. Steve was at his desk poring over some lesson plans. He looked up as he saw Edgar approach.

"So how did it go today?" he asked.

"Pretty good," answered Edgar. "They're remembering a lot of the stories. I think they really like them."

"They do. I know that for sure."

"Seemed like Chris and Jacob were okay at the end of it too."

"I hope so. You know how it is with these guys. They're pretty unpredictable. No idea what started that."

"It's probably the anger they were born with. They have no idea how powerful it is. Or even what it is or where it came from."

"Well, that's why it's good to have you here, Ed."

"I hope it helps a little bit anyways. Thanks for bringing me in here."

"Yeah no problem. I'll call you when we pin down the next date. Like I said I'm going on holidays soon so hopefully we'll get ya in before the end of the summer."

"Well, you know I'm always available. I love visiting these guys."

Edgar started getting up to go. Steve sat up straight abruptly and nervously scratched the back of his head. "Uh, before you go ... " he started. He reached into a drawer in his desk and fumbled through some papers. Edgar sat back down in his seat. Steve pulled out a piece of notebook paper, folded four times, and held it up in his hand. He swallowed hard.

"A long time ago you asked me to help you find something," he said. He scratched the back of his head and rubbed his nose nervously. "I don't know if you still want it. And I don't want to bring anything up that may be hard for you to deal with."

Edgar stared at the white, blue-lined folded sheet in his friend's hand. He felt a little lightheaded, stunned by a haunting familiarity.

"I'm not gonna say anything else about how I got it. I know just by talking and having this with me, I may be putting us both on a slippery slope. I'm just gonna leave it here on my desk. If you want it, take it. If not, I'll destroy it once you leave." Steve placed the note on the desk before Edgar. Edgar stared at it long and hard. A wave of rage and sorrow washed up his back and into his head. He had long forgotten about this request. It had been years since he made it.

Edgar reached out to touch the paper. His hand shook mildly. He nudged it open slightly with his middle finger and noticed words and numbers scrawled inside with a blue pen. He grabbed the paper with his thumb and forefinger and picked it up, bringing it slowly to his eyes. It was an address.

Edgar let out a long exhale before folding it back up and putting it in the left chest pocket of his shirt. He got up and left without looking at his friend.

He was at home that morning because he was in between jobs. He had been doing manual labour for the past two years for a couple of different construction companies in the area. Since it was winter, there were no major builds happening along the north shore, so he was collecting unemployment insurance. He was still volunteering with the Birchbark youth group, but that wasn't paying the bills. Alana wasn't working either, so she spent a lot of time with him at the Gibson family home.

Edgar got up before her and went to the kitchen to make breakfast. He turned the knob on the radio on the window-sill above the sink. The sky was thickly overcast that morning, hinting at a big snowfall to come. Because of the cloud cover, there was poor radio reception. The popular rock station from Sudbury wasn't coming in, so he turned the dial to CBC Radio just to break the still silence of the late winter morning. There was no sign of Maria yet, and he didn't really expect her to get up for school anyway. The night before, she said she wasn't feeling well. It was also a Friday. He decided just to let her be, down in her basement bedroom.

Edgar grabbed the yellow can of no-name coffee and the plastic bag of white paper filters from the high cupboard to the left of the sink. He put them beside the coffee maker at the far end of the counter, and pulled the glass pot out of the machine, taking two steps over to the sink to fill it up with water. The water swirled and bubbled in the brown-stained carafe. He turned the rusty faucet off when the water reached the line beside the "10" and walked back over to the machine to carefully pour it in the open top hatch. From the hall, he heard the bedroom door open and the bathroom door close seconds after. The shower started running.

The coffee can popped as he pulled off the plastic top. He lined the brew basket with the thin filter, and scooped in six heaps of the brown grounds. Closing the top, he pressed the "on" button, and went to sit down at the kitchen table to read the rest of yesterday's paper.

The shower stopped in the bathroom just as the phone rang. Edgar looked up at the clock on the wall beside the fridge. It was 9:13AM. He thought it was probably the office at Waverley High School, wondering where Maria was. He prepared to vouch for her supposed sickness, because in large part, he liked to dote on his baby sister. He knew he could never fill the void that their parents left, but he tried his best.

The phone was on its fourth ring by the time he stood up to answer it. He cleared his throat roughly, lifted the receiver and brought it to his ear. *"Aanii!"* he answered.

"Hello, may I speak with Edgar Gibson please," an official, monotone female voice spoke.

"Speaking," he answered.

The voice on the other end of the line softened.

"Mr. Gibson, are you the older brother of Eva May Gibson?"

He heard this official but sorrowful inquiring tone once before.

"Yes ... I am ..."

"Sir, my name is Constable Wong with the Metro Toronto Police. I'm really sorry to be calling. I'm afraid I have some terrible news..."

As he learned the details, his heart flooded with sorrow while his mind raced with malevolence.

The following Friday afternoon, Edgar, Alana and the kids were on their way back home from a shopping trip in Waverley. It was a big day. Stanley was coming home from Ottawa for a week, so Maria was making the trip down from Sault Ste. Marie as well with her boyfriend Evan. The four surviving Gibson children were reuniting for at least the weekend, which was extremely rare. They had all met at home the summer before, after Norman cleaned up. It was the first time they were all together since Stanley left for school five years earlier. They vowed then to make the summer gathering an annual event, and a year after the first one, each kept up their end of the deal.

Getting together at Christmas wasn't really in the cards for the Gibsons. Sometimes Edgar and Alana and the kids went to her rez down on Georgian Bay. Stanley often stayed in Ottawa to work over the holidays. Maria usually came back to Birchbark to spend Christmas with Edgar's family, but if he wasn't there she just went to Kathy's. Up until last year, Norman was usually nowhere to be found.

Edgar couldn't stifle his excitement. As he drove, a soft smile appeared on his face. It caught Alana's eye as she turned to the front after she checked on the kids in the back. She stared at him for a brief moment and smiled too. Lost in his own sentiments, he didn't notice as he focused on the road. She didn't say anything and looked straight ahead as well, happy that peace and joy had finally come to her husband's family.

Stanley was scheduled to get in around suppertime. He had left Ottawa mid-morning to get there on time. It was a much shorter drive for Maria and Evan, taking only about two hours coming from the West. Edgar and Alana had a big barbecue planned for that evening's meal, and grilled food like hamburgers, steak, and pickerel was on the menu for most of the rest of the weekend. They planned to spend a lot of time at the beach, along with games like horseshoes and bonfires in the backyard. Kathy and a bunch of other aunts, uncles and cousins would join them for a big supper on Saturday night. Edgar was proud to host, and he wanted to ensure everyone kept coming back year after year.

Edgar eased the van into their driveway and pulled right up to the front steps. He got out his side and went to the back to get the groceries, while Alana opened the sliding side door to let the kids out. Dylan bolted out of the van, while his mother unlocked Clara's car seat and picked her up out of it. She went around to the back and grabbed a few of the white plastic grocery bags in her free hand. Edgar struggled to lace the thin plastic loops between his fingers in an attempt to get at least five bags in each hand. Dylan went ahead to open the front door for them, and Alana led the way up with Clara in one arm and bags of food hanging from the other.

The meal preparations got underway immediately. Norman was soon home from a run, and once he showered, he was in the kitchen helping peel the corn. Edgar shaped the hamburger patties while Alana cut up onions, eggs, and celery for a potato salad. The kids were in the living room watching a VHS tape of old Disney cartoons. The adults put on the radio in the kitchen to Sudbury's rock station in an attempt to compete with the high-pitched voices coming from the TV's basic speakers. It was futile, though. The Foo Fighters' "Monkey Wrench" was pretty much inaudible. Still, the three adults worked at a steady pace, patiently awaiting their arrival of the two youngest siblings.

Suddenly the front door opened, and Maria walked through with Evan in tow. "Auntie auntie!" yelled Dylan as he jumped up and ran to hug her. "Hey buddy!" she said, leaning down to hug him. In a much more juvenile tone, Clara mimicked her brother with her own "auntie auntie" and ran in to join them. Maria stood back up with a beaming smile across her darkly tanned face. Her black hair was tied in two tight braids draped over the front of her shoulders. Despite the blue New York Knicks basketball jersey and the cutoff jean shorts she wore, she looked like a grown woman. The happiness she found in recent years added a powerful maturity to her lighter manner.

Her boyfriend Evan followed her in. This wasn't his first visit to the family home in Birchbark, but he was still shy and reserved, despite his imposing figure. Evan played hockey, and his massive physique took up most of the doorframe. He was wearing a plain white t-shirt and brown cargo shorts. His black ball cap concealed his eyes, but he respectfully took it off as he walked in the door. Edgar decided on Evan's last visit that he was a decent guy. If anything, he could protect his little sister.

Maria sauntered in and hugged them all, while Evan shook their hands. The young couple offered to help, but all that was left to do was the actual cooking. They collectively decided to move everything outside while they waited for Stanley to come in from Ottawa. Each took a bowl, plates, condiments, and cutlery and exited out the back door by the TV to set up in the yard. Edgar borrowed two large folding tables from the band office for all the food, and they already had more than enough lawn chairs to entertain outside. They laid everything down on the tables, and Edgar fired up the grill to start cooking the meat.

Soon a car pulled up on the other side of the house, and they were startled by the sound of a door closing. Excitedly anticipating Stanley, they kept their eyes fixed on the entryway. He soon appeared, and they all smiled, welcoming their brother who now clearly looked like he was a 'city Indian'. His short, dark hair was styled with gel, keeping it closer to his scalp. His small rectangular rimmed glasses had come a long way from the round monstrosities he wore as a kid. A baggy, white button-up shirt hung over his tall, skinny frame, and the silver watch around his left wrist glistened in the late-afternoon sun. His khaki shorts made his skinny brown legs look even smaller, and his sports sandals suggested comfort. They all stood up for their turn to hug him

Everyone took their seats, and Stanley sat down in the empty one beside Maria and Alana. "So how was the drive?" asked Edgar.

"Oh pretty good," said Stanley. "I'm used to it by now. I just gotta make sure I got enough tunes to make it here." Inside his rental car was a huge wallet of fifty CDs and a portable CD player attached to the car stereo.

"Did ya see any moose?" asked Norman.

"Nah, I think all the tourist traffic kept them away from the roads." Summer just about anywhere in Ontario meant weekend excursions for a lot of people. Driving seven hours just to get away for a few days as Stanley did wasn't unusual.

As the meat cooked, the siblings and their assembled partners spent the next while catching up. Stanley talked about his summer job with the government. He finished all his Master's work earlier in the spring, and soon got a four-month contract with the Department of Indian Affairs. He was unsure whether that would turn into a longer, more stable job, or whether he even wanted to stay with what was commonly known as "INAC". "We won't hold it against you ... for now," joked Maria. As the urban one in the bunch, Stanley was clearly the odd man out, but they were all proud of him nonetheless. He accomplished what he aspired to do—honour his sister Eva's legacy as a devoted student and an ambitious community servant.

Maria, meanwhile, was on her own path to solidifying a successful career. She worked in a halfway home for girls in the Soo. Most of them were Native. Because she had her own struggles with tragedy, depression, and substance abuse, she was a relatable ally and timely friend to the girls that came through the system. Most importantly, Maria loved her job, and was constantly trying to think up new ways to bring more positivity into her clients' lives. She planned on asking Edgar this weekend about setting up a sweat sometime in the fall.

The food was ready, but before everyone lined up to fill their plates, Edgar picked up a small wooden bowl from the end of the table and began to fill it with small morsels from each offering. He broke off a piece of hamburger and gently placed it in the bowl. A tiny scoop of potato salad followed, then a small chunk of grilled red pepper, and a few kernels of boiled corn right off the cob. He was making a "spirit dish"—an offering to those loved ones who have passed on to the Spirit World. This was a silent ritual. Each Gibson knew their family was well-represented in that realm. This was a small gesture to pay their respects, and to welcome the memory of their parents and sister to dine with them. Edgar placed the bowl at the end of the table, and the rest of the family lined up to feast.

They sat outside in the warm summer evening air, eating and talking until the sun went down. The four Gibsons, Alana, and Evan continued talking and catching up. Stanley and Maria got the latest rez gossip and the political on-goings in the community. Although they lived far away from Birchbark, it was impossible not to be intrigued by small-town politics. Being home was extremely comforting for Stanley. It was even more fulfilling for Edgar, the eldest sibling who had been the family leader for more than a decade. Being surrounded by his younger brothers and sister warmed his heart greatly. These moments were rare, but he revelled in them, and he hoped they did too.

As night fell and the temperature dropped, they retreated indoors. Still wired from the post-supper coffee and the excitement that came with the laughter of being around each other, they decided to stay up for a bit longer to watch movies. Dylan and Clara had gone to bed long before, so Alana opened a couple bags of chips—regular and ketchup flavoured—and put them into bowls. "There's all kinds of pop in the fridge," she said. "Help yourselves." It had been a very long time since alcohol was present in the Gibson house. Each grabbed a cold can—from cola to root beer to ginger ale—and went and sat down in the living room. Edgar walked to the TV and VCR and surveyed the cardboard cases of VHS tapes in the shelf below them. He picked out "Happy Gilmore", slid the black cassette out of the case, and shoved it into the machine.

The next day brought more family activities in stellar summer weather. They all spent most of the morning relaxing around the house. In the afternoon they went to the beach to swim and play frisbee and football. The water was calm and a darker tone of blue than the azure above. The sand was hot and radiated a cream-like shade under the blistering sun. Every so often, a supple breeze blew across their tanned bronze skin. Dylan's dad and his uncles tried to teach him how to throw a football. Stanley could catch better than he threw, so he acted as the target. Alana and Maria made castles in the sand with Clara. The faded red and blue plastic buckets were filled and packed tightly before being turned over on top of piling mounds of wet sand. The yellow and orange plastic shovels moulded and sculpted the granular structure. The collective love behind its construction reinforced it, but sadly proved no match for the wind's resilience and time's decay.

By mid-afternoon the Gibsons left the beach and walked back to the house. It took only a few short minutes, and it was a shame anyone in the family had ever driven to the beach over the years to begin with. With sand in their shoes and sandals and slowly drying shorts and bathing suits, hints of adrenaline from familial joy and reflection ran through them as they walked the dirt road. These moments of wholesome love and happiness temporarily transformed their family's legacy of tragedy.

Even greater supper preparations got underway once they got back to the house. That evening's meal was to be an even bigger reunion: Kathy and Harvey and Presley and his kids and Debbie and her family and a few other aunts, uncles, and cousins. Edgar wanted it to be like how it was at Debbie's wedding. That was the last time he and the whole family were able to sit down for a picture. It was the last time they really had a family gathering without the spectre of tragedy and loss looming over them.

Once again, Edgar got all the meat ready. He made a dozen hamburger patties to accompany an equal amount of sausages and hot dogs. He sliced three large chuck steaks into ten pieces. They expected about twenty people altogether, he reckoned. Maria helped Alana make garden and macaroni salads. The other men hovered over Edgar while he worked, offering help, but he had it all under control. They followed him out to the grill when it was time to start cooking, and just lingered in the background while the burgers seared.

By then the whole party had moved outside to await the guests. Kathy and Harvey arrived, wearing sunglasses and almost matching outfits of shorts and t-shirts. They stood out because they were both shorter than the rest of the family. Presley arrived with his four-year-old son Billy. Billy immediately rushed to play with Dylan, and Presley went over to give Stanley a handshake-hug. They were on much different paths —Stanley had been away from the community for years making a life in the city, while Presley toiled through construction jobs and unemployment on the rez—but they were still close. Presley had even visited Stanley in Ottawa a couple of times over the years. He was there the summer before to go to a Soundgarden concert in nearby Montreal.

Debbie and her husband Tim showed up with their kids. Their daughter Trisha was ten and her quick growth continually surprised Edgar. She was nearly as tall as him. Their two sons, Jordan and Mikey also joined the younger Dylan and Billy, who were playing with toy trucks on the grass. Debbie's parents Nellie and Doug were the last to arrive to round out the family gathering. Like Kathy, Nellie was the late Bill Gibson's sister.

The family chatter was loud and fast, and accelerated as the collective hunger intensified. There was a lot to talk about and many jokes to make at the expense of each other. When most of the food was eaten, Norman started piling twigs and branches on top of newspaper in the fire pit. It was still fairly light out, but he wanted to get a good start on making a huge blaze for his family. Before he started going into the sweatlodge, he volunteered as the firekeeper just to be around the ceremony.

He took great pride in that task, and that carried over to family gatherings.

The family guests left in clusters as the sun set. One at a time, they gave their thanks and well wishes before walking around to their vehicles on the other side of the house. Presley was the first to go, as Billy got tired and cranky. Soon after, the rest left, and it was just the original siblings and their spouses around the fire. Edgar's heart had blossomed over the last two days, and it was peaking now that the big supper with the family was such a success. These relatives hadn't gathered en masse like this in years, so he was proud he was able to pull it off as host. But with such elation always came a small amount of sorrow. He felt deep in his heart that Eva deserved to share in that happiness.

"So that was pretty good eh?" said Alana from her lawn chair across the fire. They sat in a circle around the flames.

"Yeah, awesome turnout, awesome food," said Stanley.

"It was really good to see everyone," added Maria.

"Yeah, it's been a while since so many of us were able to get together like this," noted Norman.

"Well, *chi-miigwech* to all of you guys for coming," said Edgar. "You've made your big brother happy. I think mom and dad would be proud."

"Yep, for sure," said Norman. Stanley and Maria nodded in agreement.

The night was silent, save for the low hum of the fire and the odd crackle of burning wood. The orange glow was intense and steady, illuminating all their faces as they sat in equidistant orbit around it. Edgar sat directly across from the two youngest siblings, and studied their young, emotionally worn faces through the flames. They reflected happiness and comfort with their faint smiles thanks to the general content of the moment, but it would take much more time to erase the traces of sorrow in their eyes.

Sitting to Edgar's right, Alana broke the brief silence. "I'm gonna go in and check on the kids and get a start on that big pile of dishes," she said. "I think I might go to bed too. I'm pretty tired." She looked at Evan to her right, who was sitting beside

Maria. It was a cue to leave the four siblings on their own to talk. He didn't get it right away.

"I'll let you guys catch up," she said more assertively, so Evan would get the hint. He looked around to see Maria and her three brothers left at the fire. He got it. "I'll go in and help with the dishes," he said. "I wanna catch the end of the Jays game too." He looked at Maria to his right for approval.

"Go ahead," Maria said. "You're a big boy." Alana stood up and walked to the stairs to go up into the house, and Evan followed. Edgar, Norman, Stanley, and Maria were left around the fire, the two oldest on one side, and the two youngest on the other. They sat for a few minutes in a comfortable silence.

"Your sister Eva would be proud too," Edgar said suddenly, picking up where he left off. To his left, Norman continued staring into the flames, while Stanley and Maria looked up at him from across. It was an unexpected statement. Just the mention of her name was enough to flare their hearts.

"She'd be proud of everything you guys have done," he continued. "She wanted this to be a good place with good people. You guys are making that happen for her." He felt a lump in his throat. Maria's eyes started to water too.

"Nah, I think she'd be complaining that she still couldn't get no fancy coffee around here," Norman joked, attempting to impede the sad tension. "Remember that time she came home for Christmas? She wouldn't even drink the homemade no-name stuff!"

Stanley chuckled, and added "Yeah, and when she really needed her fix she put so much cream and sugar in it, it didn't even look or taste like coffee!"

"It didn't take her long to become a fancy city Indian eh?" said Maria.

"She always said she was gonna come back right after she got her law degree," said Edgar. "I doubt it woulda been that quick though. She really seemed to like the city life."

"She probably woulda saved up enough for a few more pairs of shoes before she came back," said Maria. "She always talked about taking me on a shopping trip down there. Imagine the lawyer money she'd be making now!"

"No shit," said Norman. "Stan, you must make some good money with your fancy new government job. What you gonna buy us?"

"Pffff," Stanley rebutted. "I'm the lowest one on the totem pole there bro. I'm only on a temporary contract!"

"I'm just busting your balls. Buy me something nice anyway!"

Stanley chuckled and the rest smiled. Norman's face reset. "I can't believe it's been eight years already."

"Mmmmhmmm," Maria responded. Each descended into quiet reflection once again.

Edgar's hands were in the pockets of his shorts and his heart started to race. He was debating all day whether he would bring this up. It would surely draw the ire and the dejection of his younger siblings. But he believed they had a right to know. He turned over the piece of paper with his fingers a few times in his right pocket. His palms were clammy. He cleared his throat.

"I have something you guys should know about," he stated clearly and sternly. Their eyes locked on him as he paused. Norman didn't like his tone. Stanley was confused, while Maria felt a little scared. He pulled the piece of paper out of his pocket and held it up.

Like a shocking confession, he stated bluntly: "I know where he lives. This is his address."

The other three stared at the small, folded note painted orange by the fire. The blue lines became a deep purple. Edgar's hand trembled as his elbow rested on the plastic arm of the chair. "You know where who lives?" demanded Norman. Stanley felt a rage building deep in his gut. "What are you talking about, Ed?" asked Maria with a trembling voice.

"You know who I mean," he replied, shifting his eyes from Norman to Stanley to Maria. Stanley leaned forward in his chair to stare at the ground. Maria began to weep.

"What the fuck do you mean, man?" said Norman, with anger building in his voice.

"Miller," Edgar said.

"I know who the fuck you're talking about. What are you saying?

"Look, I was given this information. I'm sharing it with you. You have a right to know and here it is."

The humid summer air became heavier around them. The darkness oozed down onto their shoulders. The crackling of the fire became muffled by the anger they all felt in their ears. Each trembled, almost in unison with each other such that the restored sadness flooded their hearts and minds and became apparent in their eyes.

"Well I don't wanna fuckin' know!" shouted Maria. "I put that piece of shit out of my mind a long time ago. I never wanted to think of him again!" She put her face in her hands and sobbed.

Edgar felt tears building. Remorseful, he said, "I'm sorry Maria," and quickly shoved the note back in his pocket. "No, don't keep that," commanded Norman. "Burn it. Now."

Edgar took it back out and opened it. He looked at the street address one more time, and without hesitation squeezed it in his fist and tossed it into the fire. The small clump of paper disappeared into the burning wood and incinerated immediately.

Maria bolted up and ran past the house into the darkness, still sobbing. Norman inhaled deeply and muttered "Fuck sakes, man" as he exhaled and leaned forward. Stanley said nothing and kept staring into the grass with his fists tightly clenched. He didn't want to look at his brothers.

The next day they all acted as if nothing happened. They ate their breakfast together and carried on their cordial conversations where they left off before the reckoning by the fire. They had accomplished unprecedented familial harmony so far that weekend, and each was determined not to throw it away. Edgar regretted the moment and each of his younger siblings sensed it. They each personally vowed not to hold it against him and move on together as a family.

Stanley and Maria returned to their homes in their respective cities. Edgar and Norman carried on with life in Birchbark.

MARK
Winter 1998

Mark leaned back far in the wooden chair, feet outstretched under the table holding up an empty and a half-full pitcher of beer and three pint glasses. His friend Alex sat to his left, and his other friend J.S. sat across from Alex. The pub on Saint Catherine Street was busy and loud, and it was coming up to closing time. It was a warm refuge for a lot of drinkers on a cold Saturday night in February.

The three men in their late twenties were all very drunk. They had been at the hockey game earlier in the evening, and were bar-hopping east along Rue Saint Catherine in the direction of their various apartments. This would be the final stop on their tour, and after drinking most of the afternoon and all evening, they were sloppy and fairly incoherent.

"Fuuuuuck check out the tits on her!" exclaimed Alex, pointing obviously in the direction of a young blonde a few tables over. "Fuckin' hot!" Mark fixed his eyes on her and J.S. turned to look. "Shit man, you got no chance!" said J.S. in his thick francophone accent. Mark and Alex were anglos, and they usually all united under the banner of the Canadiens. "Fuck you, just watch!" Alex replied. He got up out of his chair and stumbled to the left, before getting his feet back under control and making a series of determined steps for a sober appearance at the woman's table. The other two watched and giggled to each other. Alex's pickup attempt was in vain and he was back at the table in under two minutes.

This routine had repeated itself many times that evening. All three were single and fairly handsome young men. Each had his share of successes. But on this particular night, their collective inebriation trumped their visual allure or makeshift charm to any women who came across them.

Mark was ready to give up. "Fuck it," he said. "I'm just gonna ... knock on that door down the hall when I get home." He pounded sharply on the table top three times, causing the empty pitcher to jump slightly. "Oh yeah, you're fuckin' that chick in your building eh?" asked Alex.

"Yeah, she's usually good to go, if she's home."

"What if she's fucking some other guy?" asked J.S.

"Then I'll kick his ass outta there!" he laughed.

"Shit man, you're probably too fuckin' wasted to even get it up," said Alex.

"Never!"

Mark picked up the half-empty pitcher and topped off all three of their glasses. They sat in mostly drunken silence for the final fifteen minutes before last call. Any attempts at starting any sort of new conversation was messy and futile, and despite the parade of alluring Montreal women that continued to stream by their table, none made a serious effort to lure them. J.S. went to the bar and ordered one more pitcher, certain to seal their wrecked fate for the end of the night.

The DJ rolled through a string of top forty hits while bodies crammed together on the tiny dance floor in front of the stage. By day and early evening this was more of a sports bar, but by night it was blasting songs like "Gettin' Jiggy Wit It" and "Tubthumping", catering to the Rue Saint Catherine Street crowd. Glasses shattered on the floor, people yelled and laughed, falling into each other. It was a sloppy scene that wouldn't appeal to anyone sober.

The songs muffled together in an audible blur and the last pitcher was empty, save for the foam that ran down inside and pooled at the bottom. Somehow J.S. managed to find a seat beside an attractive francophone woman. Alex was passing out in his seat. Mark slapped him in the chest with the back of his hand. "Wake up, fuckface!" He jerked up and his eyes opened halfway. "Let's get the fuck out of here."

The two Anglophones pushed themselves away from the table and got up. They grabbed their jackets from the back of their chairs and clumsily put them on. They both acknowledged J.S. before turning for the door, and he nodded back. Alex stumbled after his first few steps and Mark caught him. The bouncer at the door eyed them acutely as they made their way out.

Mark pushed down on the bar to open the door and stepped out into the cold winter night. The frigid air was slightly sobering for a moment. There were a few cabs parked on the street in front of them. "There you go fucker," he turned to say to Alex.

"There's your cab home."

"Aye aye captain," Alex slurred, giving his friend the middle finger before opening the back door to the one right in front of them and collapsing on the back seat. After a few seconds, the cab screeched off heading east. Mark took a deep breath and looked in both directions down the street as people started swarming out of the bars. He decided he had already spent enough money that night, so he'd walk home to save a few bucks. By his intoxicated calculation, it would only take about fifteen minutes from where he was anyway.

He put his hands in the pockets of his puffy black down jacket and started walking east. The tops of his ears were stinging already through the numbing of the alcohol, so he knew it was cold. He looked down at the bare concrete sidewalk with thick grains of salt strewn about it. He focused on his black boots, appearing one in front of the other as he marched home in the freezing Montreal night.

Mark's mind swirled randomly as he tried to pass the time in the uncomfortable cold. Clouds of moist air billowed from his nose and mouth as he exhaled. His red nose and ears were clown-like beacons on his pale white face. His brow arched downward out of frustration with the frigid temperatures. The hockey game earlier that evening had become a distant memory, as had most of the other exploits following it. All the bars blurred together, as did the weekends, and all that was left after this night of vice was one day to recover before going back to work at the auto shop on Monday. He tried to think of tactful ways to invite himself into Christianne's apartment down the hall for a late-night rendezvous.

White headlights and red taillights crammed the street beside him. Loud shouts and laughter echoed all the way up and down the strip. Mark had been out of prison for nearly half a decade. He served a little more than four years for manslaughter for Eva Gibson's death. His sentence was originally five years, but he was credited for the few months he served in custody after his guilty plea prior to his sentencing. For him, the time behind bars in Kingston Penitentiary went fairly quickly. They were uneventful years, for the most part. He was broad and tough and able to hold his own in prison. On two occasions, he was confronted by Native inmates who heard why he was there. The first time he ignored them. The second time a fight ensued. It was broken up almost immediately by guards though, and he heard nothing else about his crime from other prisoners for the remainder of his sentence.

He moved back to the Montreal area after his release. He grew up in Laval, so it was close to home. But he lost touch with most of his old friends. No one would admit it, but it was subtly intentional, even on his behalf. It's hard to stay friends with a convicted killer, and after spending years locked up, he wasn't sure how he'd relate to his former peers who had gone on to professional careers. His family welcomed him back, but by and large he just wanted to forget about the first part of his adult life.

Sometimes, though, Mark found it hard to forget about her and her family. Their faces would creep back into his conscience, especially at the most random times when his mind was in neutral, like on this particular walk home after the bar. He actually wouldn't have remembered what Eva Gibson looked like following their brief encounter at that bar in Toronto. But he saw her picture once in the paper, and the woman who kept showing up at his court appearances always held a framed picture of her. He learned after his first court date that was her aunt, and the young man with her was Eva's older brother. At each court appearance after that he tried to avoid eye contact with them, but could always feel their burning gazes heating up the back of his head.

In his youthful arrogance, he didn't believe he should have even been charged for what happened to her. It was a lapse of judgment in the heat of passion. But when it became clear that even the best lawyer his parents could hire couldn't argue past the overwhelming evidence, he had to resign himself to the fact that he'd have to plead guilty to spend less time in prison. This made him even more bitter and angry. He didn't even bother making a statement at his sentencing hearing when prompted by the judge. He believed he was just a victim himself of an unfair legal system. But when he was forced to walk past Edgar and Kathy as an officer escorted him out on that last day, he saw their sadness up close. That's when guilt and remorse first surfaced.

Those feelings grew as he was left alone with them for the first year of his sentence. They became so overwhelming at one point that he wanted to reach out to the Gibson family and say what he should have said in the courtroom that day before being led away. He thought about writing a letter. One night he even sobbed silently in his narrow cell bed.

But then other Native inmates tried picking a fight with him, and eventually succeeded. Instead of becoming angry or bitter again, he just ignored his past and tried to erase the memory of Eva Gibson altogether. It was hard to do while incarcerated, but when he got out, he vowed never to look back. There's nothing I can do about it now, he thought. All I can do is carry on with my life.

So he carried on as he did before the killing. Moving back to Montreal was an easy way to pretend that his short stint in Toronto never happened. Although the same friends weren't in his life anymore, he easily found new ones to go out and party with. His youthful arrogance and ignorance soon returned, and the privilege of being a white man in Canada allowed him to get back on his feet as though nothing had happened.

Spending the weekends drinking and partying was Mark's usual routine. He tried to shake off those bothersome old memories as he turned left to walk north on Papineau. Off the beaten strip, this street was much quieter. He usually only walked home this way when it was warmer out, but he wanted to sober up a bit in case he could score with his neighbour.

He was about a ten minute walk from his apartment building when he crossed the street to cut through Faubourg Park. It was an easy shortcut that would save him a couple minutes. The outlying snowbanks closer to the streets were painted a canta-loupe orange by the streetlights overhead. That glow dulled as he got deeper into the park, and as he walked, the constant hum of the downtown core got quieter. The February air was still, crisp, and almost peaceful. Mark looked up to see if any stars were visible. Sometimes they peeked through the general haze of urban light pollution.

Then he felt a hard thud on his back. He stumbled forward, trying to stay on his feet with the wind knocked out of him. Another hard blow to his side knocked him off the cleared concrete trail. The strikes were so sudden he didn't know what hit him. He fell to his back, looking up, and saw a dark silhouetted figure looming overtop of him. A ski mask concealed the attacker's face, but he could see the outline of its thin body against the muddy night sky above.

Suddenly from behind his head, a baseball bat came down quickly, and though Mark could hardly catch his breath, he held up his hands to block it. The crunch of his fingers meant many of them were broken. He raised his left forearm to shield himself against the next blow, and in half a second that was broken too. The attacker struck with such fury and speed that Mark couldn't think of how to protect himself. The bat came down fiercely again into his rib cage, cracking ribs and cutting his breath even shorter.

The last thing Mark heard was a muffled grunt through the mask of the attacker and the rapid crinkling of jacket material before a loud crack rattled his brain. His head went numb and he couldn't feel anything as the bat struck him in the mouth, knocking out several teeth. He lost consciousness as the next two blows collapsed his face and dark blood spurted out of his mouth and nose onto the white snow. Ten more blows shattered his skull, and as his brain swelled into the bone fragments in his head, Mark Miller was left for dead.

It was still dark by the time sleep came. The descent was rather easy, everything considered. She came in a dream.

Why?

Why did you do it?

He didn't need to die. After all this time there's no reason for revenge. You had so much going for you. You just threw it all away.

People remember me as the Indian girl who got beat up and froze to death. I died before I had the chance to leave the legacy that I wanted to. Instead, my legacy is the memory of violent death. We're tragic people. We pass on these tragedies and abuses from generation to generation. They define us. You had a chance to redefine that legacy.

Now, people are only going to remember you as the one who achieved vengeance for your dead sister. Do you think that's noble? Are you proud of yourself? You're not a hero. You hunted him down in a moment of weakness. He didn't even see you. He had no idea who you were. You didn't really make him pay because he didn't know what his death sentence was for. I moved beyond him. You should have too.

But now you're passing on that violent legacy. You're fulfilling your destiny of tragedy. I love you with all my heart. You know I do. And I know you love me too. But now hatred has tainted our relationship. Violence now defines us both. I had no choice, and I had no chance to change that. But you did. And now you've added more ugliness to my memory.

I will forgive you for this. But it will take even longer for you to forgive yourself. A long time from now, you'll have to start over. The rest of our family will have to too. This reopens many old wounds, and creates new ones. We've all already gone through so much.

You've carried on the legacy I didn't choose.

They've found his body now. They're all there, looking for you. Do the right thing.

I love you. Gi-gaawaabmin miinwaa.

He woke up with the early morning sun shining right on his face through the bedroom window. The room was cold and his nose was numb and red after just a few hours of sleep. His body, clad in a white undershirt and blue boxer shorts, was wrapped in a thick white down duvet. Despite the chill in the indoor air he slept relatively soundly in the warmth of these urban luxuries. He turned down the heat in his apartment before leaving for Montreal because he wasn't sure if he'd be heading back here right away.

He opened his eyes halfway and stared out the window. The fast-moving fireball moved quickly up out of the frame, leaving a beautiful azure in the crisp winter air. In this building, he was higher than the trees, so only the sky was visible through the small opening. He pulled the duvet up to his nose to rub some warmth into it. A healthy, faint brown tan returned to it, taking on the original Indigenous hue of the rest of his face.

Allowing himself to stay comfortable and warm for a few more minutes, he rolled onto his back to face the ceiling. He fixed his eyes on the fan above him. The three lights jutted out symmetrically from under the five blades. He counted them all in either direction—clockwise and counter-clockwise—a few times to keep his mind occupied. The odd numbers always bothered him. Instead, anything in fours seemed to put him at ease. He was never really sure why.

Finally, he threw off the heavy white covers and sat upright, settling his feet down on the carpeted floor. The thick, soft fabric tickled the soles, as it always did. He allowed himself to smile and relish the comfortable morning pattern. He vowed to take it for what it was, no more, no less. His mind struggled to stay in that routine.

He stood up and walked around the bed and out the bedroom door to the bathroom a few steps down the hall. It was a standard one-bedroom apartment in an average high-rise. The carpeted floor gave way to cold tile in the bathroom. He turned on the light on the right wall and reached straight into the tub to turn on the shower. He avoided looking into the mirror, and in the few short seconds it took to strip off his underwear, the shower was hot. Steam billowed from above the shower curtain rod, and he pulled back the translucent orange vinyl to step into the tub. It was his second shower that morning.

He went through the usual cleaning motions as if it were a normal day. He turned off the faucet and stepped out, letting the small pool of water that caressed his feet slowly drain out.

He grabbed the white towel on the rack by the light switch and began to dry off. At the mirror, he wiped the condensation clear with his right hand and looked at his foggy likeness. The steam in the small bathroom gave him a deceiving aura of divinity. His dark brown eyes seemed to cut through the misty, almost virtuous atmosphere. He stared into them deeply, as the black pupils dilated with the brown irises opening in the bright overhead electric light. The severity of his situation hit him and he shuddered before darting out of the bathroom.

He returned to his bedroom and carried on the typical daily routine of putting on clothes. He wanted to dress as comfortably as possible—boxer shorts, followed by jeans, with a black t-shirt under a cotton sweatshirt up top. Despite the cold outside, he put white cotton socks on his feet. He made sure to grab his wallet, and left the bedroom to go to the front entrance of the apartment to put on his boots and long, black leather jacket and grab his keys. He took one last glimpse into the small living room and kitchen before stepping out and locking the door.

The elevator took him down eighteen floors and released him on the ground level to face the cold winter morning outside. He pulled the black toque and leather gloves out of the pockets of his lined jacket and put them on. He pushed open the door and the sharp, frigid air blasted into his face and up his nostrils. He was already wide awake so this wasn't shocking. He turned left and walked along the sidewalk.

He reflected on his drive back to Ottawa earlier that morning. There were barely any cars on the usually busy Montreal highways as he was driving out of the city. He drove methodically and safely, keeping the car at the speed limit all the way. He stopped at a closed gas station in Vaudreuil-Dorion, and once he ensured no one was around, he pitched a black garbage bag into its dumpster. He brought it along with him to ditch the baseball bat. A twenty minute drive later, he ditched another garbage bag into a similar dumpster at another closed gas station near St. Isidore. That one had his blood-spattered jeans and canvas work jacket. Disposing of the evidence seemed moot to him now, though.

Back in Ottawa, the streets were nearly empty that early on a Sunday morning. The only vehicles he noticed on his short walk so far were cabs. Across the street he saw one woman going into her home, bundled up with a tiny dog in tow. It was cold, as it always is in February, but it didn't seem to bother him. Rather, he enjoyed the crispness of the clean air. Everything seemed to settle more easily in the winter. He took a deep breath and enjoyed the boreal freshness.

The memory of sitting around the fire last summer with his siblings flashed quickly in his mind. It would be the moment that defined the turning point of his life. It was there he learned that revenge really was possible. Again, he shook off the flashback, knowing he would have a lot of time to dwell on the decisions he made.

Once he reached Elgin Street, he turned left to walk south. He was only about a five-minute walk from his apartment, and he was nearly at his destination. He attempted to maintain a stoic and impassive resolve in the midst of this personal reckoning. But reality was seeping in, and his stomach started to feel light and queasy. He looked straight ahead, determined and focused.

He turned right to step down a brief slope that led to a high glass façade. He walked through the front doors, past the tile mural, and to the front desk. He took off his hat and gloves and stuffed them into his pockets, preparing to address the woman sitting behind the thick pane of glass. The bun of her tightly-pulled brown hair pointed to the ceiling as she looked down at some documents. Seeing her and the police patches on her uniform made him want to puke, but he choked back that unease and put his hands on the ledge in front of him. She looked up, through wide blue eyes, and asked, "Can I help you?"

"My name is Stanley Gibson," he said. "I killed a man named Mark Miller."